THE WHITE DESERT

THE WHITE DESERT

LUIS LÓPEZ CARRASCO

Translated from the Spanish by
Rosalind Harvey

GRANTA

Granta Publications, 12 Addison Avenue, London W11 4QR
First published in Great Britain by Granta Books, 2026

Originally published in Spanish as *El desierto blanco* by
Editorial Anagrama S. A., Barcelona, 2023

A CIP catalogue record for this book is available from the British Library.

1 3 5 7 9 10 8 6 4 2

ISBN 978 1 80351 177 1 (trade paperback)
ISBN 978 1 80351 179 5 (ebook)

Typeset in Arno by Patty Rennie
Printed and bound by CPI Group (UK) Ltd, Croydon, CR0 4YY

FSC www.fsc.org MIX Paper | Supporting responsible forestry FSC® C013604

The manufacturer's authorised representative in the EU for product safety is BGC Sustainability & Compliance, 7 avenue du Général Leclerc, 75014 Paris, France (gpsr@baldwinglobalconsulting.com)

www.granta.com

The ancient travel accounts will some day be as precious as the greatest works of art; for the earth was holy when *unknown,* and it will never be that again.

ELIAS CANETTI

Contents

I

THE SURVIVOR

After chatting briefly in the corridor, we entered a windowless office one by one. Indirect light, black carpet and grey walls: this is how I remember it. The head of HR asked us to take a seat around a boardroom table. In front of each of us stood a microphone (turned off), which none of us attempted to switch on. She took a deep breath and began:

'I need to give you an important piece of information. There has been a world war, which has wiped out, or will in the next few hours wipe out, all of humanity. The world as we know it has ended. The future of our planet depends on all of you gathered here now. You see that glow in the distance? That's the bombs. Just a moment, let me finish. What matters now isn't wondering how the entire population of the world has died, or thinking about your loved ones, because we're in a life-or-death situation here. We don't have much time, so you need to pay attention. You're in the basket of a hot-air balloon crossing the ocean. You managed to get into it as soon as you heard about the war, and that's how you escaped the fate everyone else has suffered. A wind has been blowing you away from the mainland for a few hours when, suddenly, you spot something in the distance. Can you see it? There, on the horizon. It's a desert island, an uninhabited island that has managed to escape the bombings. I'll answer your questions in a minute – just let me finish. It's important you bear in mind that you are the sole survivors of the entire human race. Whether or not a total extinction takes place depends on all of you here. You are the future, the seeds of a new civilization. The one snag – because there *is* a snag – is that the balloon has been losing helium for a few hours. It has a leak somewhere inaccessible that you can't repair. You have calculated that, with the current weight of the people in it, the balloon will not reach the island. It will fall into the sea, and you will all drown. Just a minute. I really am about to finish, and then you can ask me anything you want. You need to choose by consensus – this is very important – by consensus, and unanimously, which one of you must jump into the sea so that the rest can survive. One of you must sacrifice themselves so that the balloon can get to the island and humanity has a chance of surviving. I'll say it again: what's important is that this person must jump into the sea once the group has made a joint, well-reasoned, unanimous decision. It's crucial that you are unanimous. The reasons for deciding who should live and who should sacrifice themselves are based on your professions. Now, open the piece of paper you were given when you came in, and read out your skills. You must convince the others that you are necessary on this island: argue why you are essential. Remember that you are the future of a new society, and so professions that may not seem useful for immediate survival right now might turn out to be indispensable in the future. Ask me any questions before I start the timer. The balloon is deflating a little more with every second that passes.'

A young man with blond hair in a ponytail, stubble and swollen eyes chose to raise his hand rather than his voice and asked the question I would have asked, but which, out of embarrassment, I chose not to.

'What sort of bombs were they? Was it a nuclear attack? Biological?'

'That information isn't relevant for this particular role-play. What's important is the objective you've been given. What's important is that you argue and confer with each other.'

'Do we have any supplies?'

This time the person speaking was an older man in a suit and tie, the only candidate in the room who neither was in his twenties nor looked like he had a humanities degree. The rest of us adhered to the limited range of aesthetic resources which in those years characterized the university student with artistic leanings and signs of inner life: from the topknot and the horn-rimmed glasses, to the hiking boots and the piercings. A no-man's-land, as it were, between forestry and fine art. The HR woman leant back in her seat and rearranged herself in her suit jacket. She looked to be around six months pregnant.

'You have what you're carrying with you now. Of course,

your main task once you get to the island will be to find food and water. But I don't want to give you any clues!'

She must have been around forty and was all warmth and sadness. She smiled frequently, which accentuated, rather than counteracted, the general air of fatigue she gave off. Perhaps this was her aim, to stop us from bothering her. She gave the impression of having conducted countless role-plays in the 'Apocalypse balloon' format, as she had banished any spontaneity from her behaviour, and even this *but-I-don't-want-to-give-you-any-clues* seemed to have been calculated and prepared months, years ago. I wish I could remember her name – it seems like a piece of information that, at least in this particular case, would give a more rounded, accurate image of her; you would all know exactly the kind of person I was talking about. But I have forgotten it, and I'm not in a position to invent something as intimate as a name. The woman responsible for selecting the next entry-level employee for the books division of the Cultural Department Store invited her nine applicants to play, as nine embryonic professionals crossing a raging sea. Doctor. Botanist. Hunter. Fisherwoman. Carpenter. Engineer. Veterinarian. Judge. I unrolled my piece of paper: Stonemason.

'You must argue why it's necessary that you remain on the balloon. It's important you reach an agreement, although, naturally, we will also take into account whether you are the one ejected or not. It is important that you defend yourselves, that you maintain your position. You have fifteen minutes to decide who ought to die for the others, and not only that, but you must convince the one selected. You must convince them to throw themselves into the sea; you cannot use force. Start now.'

The moment the HR woman pressed the timer on her wristwatch, all the embarrassment we felt at the situation disappeared. The ridiculousness, which was individual but also collective – we were *united* in ridiculousness – the discomfort it meant to subject ourselves to an unexpected and sophisticated role-play in order to compete for a job that all those present considered badly paid, vanished at a little electronic beep. I'd like to think we all discovered that day that embarrassment can be automatically substituted for adrenaline if adequate means and appropriate recompense can be found.

'Well, what can I say? It's clear that having a healthcare professional on the island is absolutely essential. I won't be able to carry out complicated operations at first, but I'm convinced that by working with the botanical expert, I'll be able to make medicines and to take care of all of us.'

'I was about to say the same thing. I'll know which plants are edible, which have medicinal properties, which are poisonous, and I promise I'll get to work on creating a kitchen garden, somewhere we can grow things that will guarantee our survival. This is my pledge to you.'

'I don't think there's any doubt we need a hunter. At first, we'll have to feed ourselves however we can, and in this sense, the presence of an expert animal trapper is, how shall I put it, a must.'

The person who had just spoken was the young man with

the ponytail, someone who in other circumstances might have been a friend of mine. This tedious, formal tone prevailed, as if the boardroom had acquired an agency of its own, transmuted into a fully operational institutional apparatus. Caught up in ceremoniousness, we reasoned like pompous shareholders or retired senators. The brain is perfectly capable of combining apparently irreconcilable mental scenarios, and on this occasion, the imaginary danger of an imaginary death was taking place in the style of an ordinary management board meeting: the Technical Sub-delegation of the End of the World. The fisherwoman gave us food and the carpenter gave us a place to sleep. The older man with a tie held up the briefcase he had brought with him to what he must have imagined would be a standard job interview and said, solemn and red-faced:

'And I have some tools here to build the cabins, too.'

The engineer designed roads and aqueducts for us. The vet guaranteed us healthy livestock, and I saw myself plunging into a flaming sea. The judge was the weakest link, my main opponent.

'I sincerely believe that this group has a lot of potential not just to survive, but to grow and evolve as a complex urban society. I'm convinced we'll be successful. Having a person who is an expert in law, in the legal system, in private property, could mean the difference between an orderly community and chaos. My ability to mediate in conflicts may be important now, but above all, it will make things much easier in the future.'

I opened the bottle of water in front of me and took a long drink. And this is what I said:

'Dear fellow group members: I want you to close your eyes. I want you to think of the future, not in one or two years from now, but in five, ten, twenty years. A market. A paved road. Houses made of brick or stone. I want you to be ambitious, I want you to think of the needs of our shared life. I think that I can provide everything necessary for the future development of our society (*I'm speaking like this now, too?*). At first, we can sleep in the wonderful cabins the carpenter will build, but further down the line, we'll need houses that are more comfortable, more secure, more resistant. We don't know what temperature it will be on this island, what the climate's like. It will probably rain, it will probably be cold, and a cabin won't last long (*please don't feel attacked, we're a team*). Of course, the carpenter's work will always be necessary to build, erm, for instance, the tools that I'll work with. And the carts that will transport us. The engineer has great plans for us. (*Tying the knot of another alliance.*) Who will give form to her designs? Who will lay the foundations for her aqueducts? Who will find the stones for her roads? For our teammate's (*high five*) projects to have a chance of being made reality, my contribution is entirely necessary. What I mean is, if you don't have a stonemason, how will we grow, how will we build a city? Without a stonemason, who will give form to your work? (*Here I look at the engineer. Together, we form a united front.*)'

'You have ten minutes remaining.'

'Yes, but right now, what can you contribute to this group?'

The engineer untied the knot of alliance and placed the rope around my neck. Had she felt attacked? The pact of non-aggression was more than evident. I loosened the noose and improvised something, anything: a *water-treatment plant.*

'Well, now that you mention it, I can use the stones and the gravel from the beach to build a series of dams and a filtration system to make the seawater potable. In fact, erm, I think it's a project the two of us could work on together.'

The hunter spoke up from the other side of the room:

'The odds are we'll be able to drink water from a stream. Why would we build a thing like that?'

'But we don't know that. What's important here is that we don't know anything about the island. We don't know how big it is, we don't know if there are trees, if there are mountains, if there's fresh water. (*Reasonable doubt, reasonable doubt, hold on to reasonable doubt.*) This is why we have to think about which of us is the most versatile, in the short as well as the long term.'

'I think we should vote. Let's see. Who thinks the stonemason is the least necessary?'

It was the judge dealing me the knockout blow. Five of them raised their hands, all except the fisherwoman, the botanist and the carpenter. I requested the floor:

'Let's all calm down a bit, please. Do you really think a stonemason is less important than a *judge*? Seriously? Is the division of land or an inheritance more important than a bridge, a market, a whole city? Even if you don't think a stonemason's vital, please take a moment to think about when you are going to need a judge. And in any case, without a stonemason, the presence of the engineer is totally useless.'

Rumbling, outrage, a riot of voices. Suddenly worked up,

everyone had something unique to contribute to the future. Entire civilizations were imagined in seconds: kingdoms of carpentry, fruit-tree architectures, fish-scale coins, the Mesolithic in its entirety completed in a decade. I realized my mistake. I had started too many battles, too many lines of attack, made too many enemies at once; after the hubbub, they would regroup and pulverize me. The judge's half-smile, calm and confident, constituted an enigma I still have not resolved, and will not. With her short, curly blonde hair, she had admitted to us when she arrived that she had just been hired by a rival bookshop – located in a large department store constructed during the final years of the dictatorship – where they paid better, even though they would make her wear earrings and make-up. She had decided to turn up for the role-play for the Cultural Department Store because she had nothing better to do and was killing time while waiting for a friend to come and meet her. Nothing better to do than destroy me and, while she was at it, throw me into the sea. As good a way as any to 'kill time'. I believe her name was Olga. After this pause, I observed how the most fragile professions strengthened fanciful alliances. A wooden lift had just been constructed, manufactured exclusively with words. On the other side of the table, of the basket, of the island, an electric generator was giving off its first sparks thanks to the aeolian force of a few fish fins. Seven minutes left. Nervousness. Real, collective, contagious nervousness. Someone *pointed at me*. The engineer, who had scaled new heights of chutzpah, argued that she alone was capable of building her designs. Along the way, we had regressed from the considered arguments of earlier; rudimentary craft sessions now counted as evidence:

'When I did my degree, we had practical sessions, too, and I built one of those dams for filtering potable water with my own hands.'

Stealing the water-treatment plant that I had invented – conjured out of thin air – ought to be considered an irrefutable indicator of desperation. Or of hatred. I looked around me. Hunter, fisherwoman, doctor, botanist. Invincible. Vet? We would need livestock. But what if there were no animals capable of being – what do you call it – stabled? Should I say this phrase in public? Wouldn't it sound a little bit ridiculous? The carpenter could be easy prey (*these cabins will fall down, you're going to need my patience in construction, my foundations; I am the foundations of this future society, etc.*), but I felt sorry for him – a confused, sweaty gentleman, with his blazer, tie and wristwatch, his bald head reflecting pale flickers of light from the fluorescent bulb above him.

'Do you really think the presence of a judge is more important than solid buildings that can withstand the passage of time?'

'I think a judge is important. There might be bad vibes, arguments. A court is the bedrock of civilization.'

This was the view of the young man with the ponytail and goatee, round glasses, a pendant with an arrowhead or some sort of Celtic symbol hanging from it, trousers with a copious amount of pockets and a yellow T-shirt with the likeness of a well-known Rastafarian on it; this was his view, sprawled in his seat, unassailable with his innate hunting skills. The reggae fan. When the HR woman informed us that we had only five minutes left, the clamouring stopped; a silence fell. I believe I can say for sure that we were all listening to the sound of waves, the black clouds, the silent mass of land that could be glimpsed through the heavy rainfall. We would plunge into the depths if no one jumped. The vote was repeated. Aside from the carpenter and the vet, everyone was against me, the stonemason. The vet, with sound judgement, asked them all to let me speak. I peeped over the edge of the wicker basket and saw the dark sea, thunderous, ready to swallow me up. There was a flash of lightning. Adrenaline quickened my pulse. (*Reasonable doubt, reasonable doubt.*)

'One thing. There's one thing we haven't considered. I think we're all in agreement that we are all necessary on this island. It might be that, as a stonemason, I am the least necessary person at this moment and in years to come. It's true that the judge may be fundamental from the beginning of this, erm, new society. We're taking it for granted that we'll all have a purpose and I agree, I agree with it all except for one thing. Do we know what the island is like? Do we know how big it is, if it has valleys, if there are forests? We're taking for granted that there'll be fresh water, and I really hope that is the case, but what happens if there aren't any animals? It wouldn't be unusual if on this little stretch of land all that's left are insects. Hang on a moment, I'm speaking. I don't doubt there'll be plants, I don't doubt there'll be fish. But if there are no animals, a hunter would be completely redundant. I'm not saying there won't be turtles turning up to lay their eggs, but I don't think you need a hunter to steal a few turtle eggs, am I right? There'll be one member of the community who would have literally nothing to do.'

How can there not be any animals, we'll starve to death, well, we'll eat fish, then, well what happens if there isn't any fish, but how can there not be fish, seriously, so what about the vet, then, the vet's a kind of doctor, though, but in that case we have two healthcare professionals, you can never have too many doctors on an island, well then, what about the carpenter, what's the carpenter got to do with all this, the judge needs to settle this, but I know how to hunt, I know how to hunt all kinds of things, you'll see, I promise.

'You have three minutes left.'

I advanced a little further with my strategy: to attack the one who was beyond all doubt.

'And I'll tell you something else: the hunter won't have much to do either once we begin *stabling* the animals, don't you think?'

The guy with the topknot began to shake. He hated me, he hated me intensely. Would he fall into the trap I had set for him? He looked at me as if I were an idiot and, practically shouting – or howling, rather – took aim:

'And what if there *are* wild animals, eh? Who will protect you all if there are *big cats*?'

I pulled the rope tighter before he could escape.

'And what are you going to use to kill wild animals, big cats, if all we have is what we've got with us right now?'

At that – and I promise you that this really did happen – the young man leapt up from his seat in a total frenzy, and after struggling to undo the zip on one of his many pockets, shaking and stammering, eventually plunged his hand in, ecstatic and victorious, and showed us what he held gripped in his fist as he yelled at me: 'My knife! With this knife! You see it? With this knife I'll hunt for you all!'

There was nothing in his hand. There was nothing *visible* in his hand, I mean, given that, as he shrieked, he shook this nothing, this nothing *in the shape of a knife*, and pointed at me with it – in a frankly threatening manner – as proof of his hunting prowess. In his confusion – I realize now as I write these lines, so many years after this happened – he had also had obvious difficulties in getting this imaginary knife out of his pocket, which leads me to venture the following hypothesis: the imagination, too, is subject to the individual's physical strength and stamina.

After a few seconds, terrible and devastating, of silence, uneasiness, embarrassment and ridicule – all, once again, felt collectively – the carpenter offered to 'sharpen a few sticks' for the hunter to use as spears. Then came the moment for us to vote, and they unanimously decided to give me the boot. The woman from HR, the mistress of ceremonies, looked at me without seeing me – her mind somewhere far away, floating in a different balloon to ours – and, in another unexpected twist, offered me the chance to say a few Last Words. I bid them a friendly farewell and wished sincerely that everything would go well for them. Then, I said goodbye and threw myself into the sea. A selection process combining (dramatic) role-play, the frenzy of survival and the verbose language of a board meeting required, without a doubt, some element of death. Immediately after, we were informed that we would be notified of the results by phone and we left the place, awkward, hushed and a little saddened, as when you share a secret you wish you'd had no knowledge of.

Once outside, I said a vague goodbye to my fellow interviewees. It was an April evening, unusually warm for Madrid. I was on my way to Aitana's apartment when I heard a distorted, amplified voice, the voice of a woman at a microphone cutting out and crackling from the volume being too loud. Some way off, in Puerta del Sol, a stage and a huge screen had been set up. The screen was so enormous that even at this distance I could make out the face of Irene Villa. On the stage, at the foot of the screen – that is, at the foot of the face – I saw a tiny little figure, the person who up until very recently had represented the savage, cruel and wanton violence of ETA.* I

* Today's readers may not recall who Irene Villa was – and even ETA may only ring a faint bell. ETA, Euskadi Ta Askatasuna, was a terrorist group in Spain which generated mass fear. Villa was a survivor of one of their many attacks. In 1991, at the age of 12, Villa, along with her mother, was the victim of a car bomb which separated both her legs and one of her hands from her body. Exceptionally gory images from the attack were broadcast on television, along with Villa's subsequent experiences of overcoming the attack both psychologically and physically. Her story became a symbol of the struggle against separatist terrorism, as well as of the pain of its victims.

walked towards this event, intrigued. As I passed in front of the large late-Franco-era department store where Olga, the judge, would soon start work in the books department, I was struck by the sense of familiarity, peaceful and calm, that these shopping centres had always given me. An outmoded feeling of serenity, not at all desirable, but from which I have never felt able to escape, either: each and every afternoon of my childhood was spent queuing up with some schoolfriend or other to play the video games on display or, a little later, to listen to records for free or look at posters for our bedrooms. Too many objects triggering the mind to play tracks from my memory for me to avoid this childish, teenage, and yet largely inoffensive feeling of attachment. Back then these shopping centres still served as a decidedly recognizable place, permanent in time and perfectly reproducible in space – all the provincial capitals had them, and they were all exactly the same – which now, after all these years, seems to me to be the only truly imperturbable location that ever existed in the whole country. In any unknown city, strange and unwelcoming, you could walk down the long aisles of the department store, past counters and window displays stacked high, and feel 'at home'. Only the consumerist dream of Francoist entrepreneurship was capable of producing the identitarian illusion of an immutable, long-lasting geographical identity. A toyshop where you could get your hair cut, a delicatessen where you could try on a bikini, a bookshop where you could reserve three nights in a hotel, a jeweller's where you could watch, multiplied and synchronized, the faces on the news bulletins in cascading rows of televisions. A familiar past-tense universe that pre-dated the birth of the young democracy surrounding us, a place where you could acquire your tie and your perfume, your moisturizer and your blouse: the place of gifts, the dangerously cosy world of our grandparents.

Halfway down the street I could clearly make out the amplified face – its dimensions matching those of the offices of the regional government – of the country's most famous victim of terrorism, preparing to give some kind of speech to a crowd that was slowly filling the square. Little heads with straw hats holding pale blue balloons; a tender swell. I distinctly recall thinking in that moment how different the future was to how we had imagined it – or to how it had been imagined for us by films, comic books, video games and other fictions. A face on a screen the size of a building was an iconic image in the science fiction half-seen in childhood and evoked a whole spectrum of gloomy yet alluring scenes: rainy metropolises, flying cars, floating screens, celestial PA systems. Electronic screens on metro platforms were still a novelty at that time, and the façades of the buildings on Gran Vía were not yet covered over with blinding screens: if this gigantic image, suspended above our heads, had any corollary, it was to a mysterious future of cold neon lights and stormy avenues glimpsed in a childhood dream. But, with the first decade of the twenty-first century having only just finished, the future seemed to have been postponed until further notice. Or perhaps it was here before me, brought forward in time, and was little more than a pale echo of the images seen on screen.

All the elements were there, but badly assembled or clumsily juxtaposed: a large metropolis, technological spectacles, an anonymous mass of people, the surge of traffic, touristy commerce and commercial tourism. The liquid crystal display against the Herrerian granite, the electric scooters clattering across the paving stones, the pedestrians from faraway countries relaxing alongside monarchs on horseback, while people dressed in cartoon-character costumes danced around under the sun together with the woman giving foot massages, the charcoal caricaturist and the galactic mime artist. The megaphone from the event blared out loudly, drowning out the roar of the traffic, and the dazzling screen with a resolution of millions of DPI shone as brightly as the sun. There was Irene Villa, surrounded by families, but above all by old men and women. On the little flags and balloons were the slogans 'Yes to Life' and 'Defend Life', along with the logos of the country's main right-wing newspapers and radio stations. The issue with the sound seemed to be resolved now, and the woman, who could have been my older sister, read out – shaking a little at first, although she very quickly recovered, growing proud and fervent – a speech against euthanasia and abortion. 'If a law permitting euthanasia had existed in 1991, I would not be here with you all right now.' Science fiction and Catholic fundamentalism looked to be in rude health from where I was standing.

Aitana wasn't at home, and her flatmate, sleepy and pot-bellied, was eating spaghetti at six in the evening. He did PR for a nightclub and went to bed first thing in the morning. 'Every day is an afters. In every sense. I'm always late to the party.' Even the spaghetti he had eaten cold, distracted by a phone call. They lived on a narrow street behind Jacinto Benavente, a thirty-five-square-metre apartment with windows looking out onto a minuscule patio that, due to some miracle of orientation, reflected the sun almost all day long thanks to its whitewashed wall, which you could touch if you stretched out your arm. What can we have talked about that day, Aitana's flatmate and I? I don't remember. I remember going into her room, lying down on the bed and stroking their cat, Micaela, an upmarket pet they had been gifted because she had problems related to dwarfism and would die if she ever fell pregnant. An exclusive breed, genetically designed to be a companion animal, she had no real muzzle to speak of, which meant she suffered from respiratory problems. A clumsy, angelical presence, extraordinarily placid, she would be incapable of surviving outside the domestic environment. The desk in Aitana's room was covered in piles of notes, scrupulously organized by subject and separated by folded sheets of A4 or in branded folders from the university's photocopying centre: we were in the last year of our degrees and about to enter the exam period. A year later we would move in together. One corner of the desk, near the headboard, acted as a bedside table, and there I counted two almost-empty packets of rolling tobacco, some tissues and a photo of Aitana with her father. Her entire family came from a few tiny Asturian villages, and she had been able to come to Madrid to study thanks to the travel grants

Zapatero* had just pulled the plug on due to the economic crisis of the previous year. At that time, she was juggling her classes with various jobs and some paid internships at the radio station, which she hoped to extend into the summer with a temporary contract. She was the second person in her family to go on to higher education; the first was a distant cousin who worked as a paediatrician in Valladolid. In the photo, she and her father were smiling in Madrid's Plaza Mayor; she had just arrived in the capital, and her hair was still long and brown, and I didn't yet know her. Aitana's father, a boyish, good-natured man, had been on the verge of being the Socialist Party's mayoral candidate in their village, although at the time of the photo, he had been pensioned off due to a work accident while maintaining the northern narrow-gauge railway line. I heard a door slam; it was Aitana. I came out into the hallway, which was also the living room. I remember that at the time she had her hair cut short and bleached, a sparkling blonde. (We all wear it closely cropped now, including our daughters; it's what's most comfortable here.) She was breathing hard – not because of the heat, but because of the rage she was in. She shrugged off her rucksack and set down a couple of bags of papers and office equipment. She swore and cursed at somebody, and I realized that they hadn't renewed her contract at the radio station; I stood there frozen, not knowing what to do. I thought she was going to hug me and

* José Luis Rodríguez Zapatero was president of the Spanish government from 2004–2011, and a member of the Socialist Workers' Party of Spain.

cry from rage or frustration, but no, she didn't cry. She asked me to turn on the laptop while she rolled a cigarette; neither she nor her two fellow interns were to be kept on. At that time, it was sometimes preferable when it came to jobs in advertising or broadcast media to not finish your degree so that your employment status would still be that of an intern. The agreements prohibited the hiring of students who were no longer enrolled – by that point they counted as 'workers' – and so lots of young people would put off doing the final exam for one module until the possibility of a temporary contract with an agency, newspaper, radio station or TV channel arose. Needless to say, this hardly ever happened, and so there was a cycle of old interns being replaced by eager new students, gagging for employment. Aitana had in any case decided to graduate in June, but then the possibility had arisen to go for a *real* job covering for the producer of a culture show that went out at midnight – 'culture' was a profoundly nocturnal matter when it came to the programming policy of this particular station. Since the other two interns were not going to finish their degrees, it was entirely feasible that they would stay on as interns while Aitana, once she had graduated, would fill the empty position, which would last for as long as the producer – a woman Aitana barely knew – chose to remain on maternity leave. We were, in effect, following the development of this late first pregnancy – the woman must have been around forty-two – with a certain amount of self-interest. The sooner she started her leave, the more months of work Aitana would get. She had spent the last two weeks preparing references from her previous employers – she had done work experience at national radio stations every summer, and also used to produce and present a programme about immigration and human rights for a local channel – in order to apply for a role which she was in fact already doing.

On the modest screen of the laptop, no more than the size of a sheet of A4, a young woman's CV sparkled. Twenty-three years old, blue eyes, white shirt, shoulder-length light brown hair. 'This is who they've given the job to. I had a look and found her CV. Look at her! A degree from some godawful university, look, look at the work experience she's got: two months at the university radio station, and a year ago she ran the social media accounts for . . . her dad's company! Can you believe it? Where on earth has this posho come from? What the fuck is going on? She's never worked a day in her life, privileged little brat. How can a professional radio station hire someone like this? Who made this decision? Who do they owe a favour to? The station's not even religious, or right-wing – why on earth are they getting someone from a private university? The heads of programming, the women in HR – they all value my work . . . So, who makes these decisions? If they'd gone for someone with more experience than me, I wouldn't care, but to go for absolute mediocrity? Look, she's got one of those old Castile surnames, like a marchioness from Burgos. Fuck me and the Catholic Monarchs! How far do the connections of these people extend, Carlos? All the way down to a crappy entry-level contract, that's how far. It's not even about me, it's about the job, the show, my colleagues – why should they be lumbered with this waste of space? The station's gone to shit, the shows suck, and the unions are totally fucked, run by an army of rich kids with the right connections. Why would any of them make a change if they were all hired as a favour? I'm not surprised this country's gone to shit, I'm really not. I'm not surprised we're in the doldrums. I'm not surprised we've got a load of petty fucking tyrants as our overlords. It makes sense: we deserve it, for being mediocre, mean-spirited cowards. We're ruled by idiots, we're managed by idiots, we're employed by idiots. You know what? I hope this whole country crumbles. I hope we all get out of here, leaving those vile fuckers to deal with their own shit as it all goes down the drain – all the fucking way. It's true, I really do think that sometimes. It'll serve them right. I hope this country goes down the drain and takes them with it! You hear me? Down the fucking drain!'

I struggle to remember the details of the rest of that day. I guess we must have gone out, had a few beers in the bars that weren't yet overrun with tourists, met up with some friends, the kind who are always in a good mood. At some point I got a phone call to give me the good news that I'd been selected for the bookselling job. I was due to start the following week. I think I thought that perhaps the woman from HR hadn't told us the whole story, and that the person who threw themselves into the sea was the one who would get the job in the end. I said nothing to Aitana until the following day, out of embarrassment or tact. That's how I got my first job.

*

More than two decades have passed since then, and now those places – Madrid, Spain – are completely inaccessible to me for a whole host of reasons, and so I don't know if Aitana's prophecy came true altogether or only in part. It is hard to find out; the information we get here is patchy at best. It's easy to distrust the news when you're so far away. When I read back over what I have written, I wonder if I might have mixed up a few pieces of information, a few facts, and if there are perhaps some incidental or irrelevant passages. I've merely attempted to write it all down just as I remember it. I thought that by doing so I'd be able to travel for a few moments to the place where I lived for so many years of my life – and to which, for reasons we all know very well, we cannot return – but that didn't happen. I'll admit to you now that by writing it down I haven't relived it, nor have I remembered it any better.

And I read a curious phrase, too:

'. . . electronic screens on metro platforms were still a novelty at that time, and the façades of the buildings on Gran Vía were not yet covered over with blinding screens . . .'

I wrote 'covered over,' which might not seem like the best phrasing. Nonetheless, that is what occurred to me, and when I ask myself why – why didn't I simply write 'covered with', which might sound more appropriate – I can't help but think that those screens, sharper than human vision and brighter than any public lighting, covered over something that was there before and that, since their installation, was no longer there. No, 'to cover over' is absolutely not the same as 'to cover'. They enveloped the city in shiny wrapping paper and ever since that moment it couldn't be anything other than a gift in our eyes. Who was it meant for, this gift our city had become? We hoped it was for us, because who can live inside a gift meant for someone else? I no longer recall what there was before the wrapping paper, and so there are holes in this scene. There is a part I cannot remember for you all.

II

OCEAN OF LIGHT

Jimena Sánchez Bravo's plane, Emirates* flight 202, took off for Sydney on the morning of 4 September 2019. She had just made an early-morning stopover in Dubai, her memory of which will consist of the tap water in the bathrooms being scalding hot and the passengers all congregating around the shops and restaurant franchises, hyperactive and manic. When I eventually called her so she could tell me what had happened – after making sure that she had completely recovered – she told me she was surprised that no one was sleeping. On other trips, she had made night-time stopovers in big airports, in London, Zurich, São Paulo, and there was always a certain amount of activity in the terminals, but this was different. No one looked sleepy or lethargic, not a single

* Emirates was a well-known passenger and cargo airline. Owned by the government of Dubai, it was the largest airline in the Middle East, and one of the most important in the world.

yawn could be seen along the rows of seats. Not one businessman's head nodded, not one baby stopped crying. There was a sense of agitation in the air, a tireless pulsing, as if time zones had been done away with and there was no separation between night and day. She would only see the city as they were leaving it behind: an army of skyscrapers emerging from the sand, hazy in the dust-filled air. The sky almost as yellow as the soil, the horizon perfectly neutralized. Her ex had lived there before they met and she still had some remnant of curiosity about the place – she didn't actually mention this last detail when we spoke, but I'm sure it was on her mind. On the plane she was finally able to sleep a little, a couple of hours at most, from which she emerged calm and rested – excited, even, about the trip. She took advantage of this welcome enthusiasm to go over her talk: the following day she was due to give a paper at an international veterinary conference on the results of the previous semester's research into IFI detection techniques for feline leukaemia virus. When she closed her laptop, it must have been around midday. She looked out of the window and saw a vast mass of water gleaming, blurring into the sun itself; the radiant ocean all around them. The person sitting next to her, an Australian man of around seventy, asked if it was her first visit to his country. She said that it was and he, affable, asked her about the document she has been working on. The man was dressed in the comfortable, slightly dishevelled style of those who have travelled too many times with a business suit on when they held a position with some degree of prominence. Jimena was put in mind of a retired diplomat when she looked at his wrinkled linen shirt, his khaki-coloured Bermuda shorts, the socks with sandals. Her seatmate possessed many of the features we associate with a certain kind of stereotypical English-speaking male: patrician head of hair, frank jaw, mischievous expression, glacial hands. The friendly colonel, the unruffled explorer. They chatted for some time, around an hour, which leads me to imagine that she must have explained in quite some detail various aspects of her research. I am not sure, however, if they got around to talking about him – I think at most, this gentleman, whose name we will not find out, would have given her recommendations for places to visit in Sydney – but they were sufficiently focused on their conversation not to notice what was going on around them.

Knowing Jimena as I do – even though it's been a while now since I have spoken with her; ever since Aitana and I left, we can no longer call each other on the phone – my guess would be that she began like this:

'It's a presentation on an academic study on the characteristics of an immunostaining technique – that is, the labelling of certain antibodies in order to demonstrate the recent presence of a specific antigen in an organism, an antigen that has caused a disease. Specifically, we're working with SIF detection methods: secondary (indirect) immunofluorescence. This is a kind of immunolabelling that uses antibodies chemically bound to a fluorescent substance, which means we can clinically demonstrate the presence of a certain antigen microorganism – in this case, feline leukaemia virus. We're analysing how precise this technique is in infected maternal milk. Cat's milk, naturally. It's a pilot study, but at some stage it can be applied to similar secretions from other animals. We're making use of the capacity antibodies have to bind to a specific target molecule; in this study we label the antibody with Fluorescein isothiocyanate. The labelled antibody is made to react against a biological preparation and is then exposed to a short-wave light source – for example, ultra-violet – which produces a fluorescent phenomenon in the labelled molecule; this then emits light at a longer wavelength, such as yellow or orange. This light can reveal the location at a cellular or sub-cellular level of the target molecule. The SIF is a somewhat complicated test and it's more likely to suffer from interference, because it combines two antibodies instead of one, although it's also far more flexible than a direct immunofluorescence technique, due to the fact that it's possible a primary antibody bonds to more than one secondary antibody; this enlarges the sample, which means we also enhance the sensitivity of the detection technique . . .'

I imagine that at some point the Australian gentleman would have enquired about the well-being of the cats, and the conversation would have moved on to more relatable, uplifting areas. It's not my intention to give the impression that Jimena did not take her interlocutor's sensibilities or courteous nature into account; rather, only that she has always been someone who is passionate about her work.

*

It was the gesture that interrupted them, the firm gesture of the head flight attendant as she rebuked a woman who had started screaming. It wasn't so much the scream as the gesture, imposing and unexpected, that caught their attention, and not for its violence, but rather for its authority. It turns out, we find it more surprising – and hence think it more inappropriate – that an air hostess might tell a customer off than that this customer is shouting, crying, hurling insults or stamping their foot. Meanwhile, the rest of the crew – exquisitely calm and polite, prompted by the need to pretend nothing was happening – asked the passengers to put their seat backs up, stow their tray tables, and put their seatbelts on. The windows grew dark – no doubt to stop passengers from seeing the inevitable smoke and flames. Jimena recalled seeing the engine burning, but also wasn't sure if she had made this up. She did remember, without a doubt, the explosion. It wasn't until everyone was bent over their knees, anxious, praying, and, as such, *receptive* to a less peachy update, that the captain announced over the tannoy that he would 'try to make the forced landing as smooth as possible . . . The island has a wide sandy cove where we can perform the manoeuvre.'

Losing altitude causes a sort of mild dizziness, as if someone were singing you a lullaby; I recall these words of Jimena's over the phone, but I have no way of knowing if her face was expressing warmth or coldness as she said it. I imagine it a nightmarish lullaby, filled with shaking and death as the plane hurtled towards the sea. Someone screamed again and was quickly shushed by the other passengers, who had evidently found some kind of assurance in the silence, in the sense of resolution it inspired. This was how the crew and passengers of Emirates flight 202 faced the emergency landing on an unknown island in some part of the Indian Ocean: in silence, as if in prayer. It was then that the explosion in the left engine happened, and a deafening noise washed over everything.

They come crawling out, very slowly. The sand is soft and white. Everything is white. They go a few metres and then drop down, exhausted. There is nothing but light around them.

Slowly the green appears. A dense canopy of palms. Slowly the noise reappears, an echo of the deafening hurricane their lives have become, lives in which the last few minutes have been experienced as if they were years. Has this noise become lodged inside them forever? It is true that the noise will remain with them – although transformed, as time goes by, into the waves of the sea. The blue of the sky arrives, the smell of vomit arrives. And so, they vomit once again. For another few minutes, all that can be heard is rhythmic retching, as if they were taking it in turns to be sick. Pain arrives; it is generalized and difficult to pinpoint. But the pain returns them to themselves. Jimena remains in the foetal position. She stays like this for an incalculable amount of time. The sun, bright and insistent, bothers her. Slowly, she sits up and sees all the passengers filling the beach; six hundred people all curled up, seemingly asleep. The plane is there in front of them, and Jimena gazes at it fondly. She sees it as a prehistoric animal that has protected them, saved them, and now lies dying. The fire burnt itself out before reaching the fuel tank. The port-side wing is black, the landing gear cracked. The aircraft swerved at the last minute and now has its back to the sea, muzzle pointing towards the jungle. She tries to speak but doesn't quite dare; everyone appears to be asleep, and in any case, she is almost embarrassed, as if she doesn't really know what her voice will sound like or whether it is to be trusted. She stretches a little, takes off her jacket. The sea breeze feels pleasant on her skin, it's a welcome relief from the power of the sun and somewhat helps to wash away the smell of vomit, which Jimena hopes she has left behind on her blazer. By the plane, some movement is visible – the flight attendants are helping an old woman climb out. She appears completely unharmed; she takes a few steps, then sits down on the ground. Their task completed, the flight attendants slowly sink to the ground, until they are on their knees, leaning against the fuselage, without even the energy to lie down properly. Jimena could be using this time to assist someone who is badly wounded, but she doesn't want to move or ask questions – she doesn't want to trigger any thought, worry or fear. Getting up would mean setting time and responsibility into motion. Getting up would mean becoming an adult again. They all deserve a rest, not just from the accident, but from something more, too.

But as soon as the first question appears in her mind, she is compelled to get up. Naturally, this first question is: where are we? Although she isn't able to answer it, and though it vanishes as quickly as it appeared, it breaks the spell, propelling her into worrying about the physical well-being of the rest of the passengers.

They must have been very numb and shell-shocked still, because none of them remembered feeling glad when the captain informed them that no one had died or been seriously injured. There's no applause or hugging; instead, they start looking around, as if suddenly their surroundings are now worthy of a more detailed examination. The crew walk over to the cabin to try and re-establish communications and send for help, while all the people with bruising and slightly more ostentatious injuries sit down near the emergency exit and wait to be seen to. The head flight attendant selects a few passengers to go with her to see if the food and drink on board is still usable. Everyone remains very close to the plane, occupying the large open space of the beach in a way that appears absurd, to say the least. Half a thousand people all crammed together, very close to one another, chatting, smoking, fanning themselves, as if they were still in a terminal or on a platform, waiting to be transported somewhere else, while the rest of the beach remains empty, untouched. Somebody shouts. A deep male voice. A few other voices, female this time. They aren't cries of fear; they are directed at something. Jimena moves away from the crowd to get a better look. They are shouting after a couple walking away from the group down the beach. A man and a woman, both young, moving slowly along the shore, not speaking to one another. The man with the deep voice runs towards them. He shouts at them in English to come back. Each lost in their own thoughts, they only notice him once he has almost caught up with them. Perhaps they don't understand English so well. They begin to head back towards the group, sad and dejected, not understanding what they have done wrong. The man who had chased after them, his hairline receding sharply and his shirt buttoned up incorrectly, huffs in a British accent:

'Who do they think they are, these two – do they think we're on some island retreat?'

The beach is, without a doubt, a paradise: the sea calm and turquoise, the sky clear, dotted with only a few white clouds. Behind them, hundreds of coconut trees, some bent over towards the ground, as if offering themselves up as seats or deckchairs. It is still too early for them to dip their toes in the water, but soon they will do so. The crew does not know for certain which island they are on, but they have assured everyone that it is uninhabited. Jimena still doesn't feel like talking to anyone, and she hasn't been able to do much as a medical professional, either – her entire life has been dedicated to research. She could put a splint on a broken leg if it came to it, but not much more. No one has asked for her help, though. There have been a few cut foreheads and split lips, but, otherwise, the biggest frights have come from people with heart pain or breathing trouble, all of which have turned out to be anxiety attacks. The anguish lasted as long as it took to find the appropriate medication in the first-aid kit. More voices are heard: the young man from the couple who'd walked off down the beach, dressed in a djellaba, is confronting the older man who ran after them. His wife, in a hijab, needs a wee. The situation, awkward and unpleasant, reminds them that they haven't rid themselves of future violences, either. A few groups head into the forest to answer the call of nature, while a segment of people (all white) insist that no one should do anything until they have asked for permission from the captain. The head flight attendant comes over to where the commotion is and settles the matter with a wave of her hand. 'Just don't go too far.' The older man with the deep voice mutters and plots: 'She didn't actually go and talk to the captain, it's so reckless. I think we should go and tell him what we think, that no one should move from here.' Jimena walks down to the shore, eager to freshen up, but also eager to annoy this bunch of idiots. The sunshine glints off the waves, comfortingly; a sparkling trail towards nowhere. She slips off her shoes and walks in up to her ankles. She is the only one to do so. She is about to take another step, but senses disapproving looks boring into her back. Is she putting herself *in danger*? She knows that if she takes another step she will hear the furious, panicked voice of that insufferable bloke again. In any other situation she wouldn't have cared and would have taken that second step, but a wave of weariness reminds her she is more depleted than she thinks. Better to conserve her energy for later – for who knows what might happen.

For what might happen. In any other situation. After all, what situation are they in? Is it an accident? Are they lost? Shipwrecked? How to classify a situation like this, such a textbook example from children's storybooks and adventure stories? How many books and films set on desert islands has she herself enjoyed in the past? Can these fictions be of any use to her now? She suddenly takes a step back – perhaps because the wind changes, perhaps because a little strip of cloud briefly obscures the sun. She hasn't seen anything, but nor has she seen nothing, either. The water is crystal clear and she doesn't detect any movement; there is nothing that can bite or attack her, but the sensation of danger ripples through her regardless. She turns around slowly and heads back up the beach, feeling like she has been defeated by something, even if she doesn't yet know what it is.

'We suggest you always stay in pairs or groups! Do not go into the forest alone – there might be animals!'

The head flight attendant is speaking from the top of a rock. Next, she asks for volunteers to help her remove trays of food from the plane. The water has been distributed and Jimena has already stepped on a few empty bottles, crushed and partially buried in the sand. Someone puts their hand up amid the throng, but she is unable to hear the question.

'They're asking if we can go and get our luggage, so we can change our clothes and grab some of our personal belongings. Lots of people have . . . you know, soiled themselves,' says a gentleman next to her, a girl of around eight on his shoulders. 'It was my daughter who heard the question,' he tells her, brimming with pride at the girl's acuity. Their names are Arash and Fairuza, although Jimena will not find this out until later.

The head flight attendant, their unflagging leader, organizes a group of twenty people to empty out the hold. Jimena surprises herself by pushing people aside to join the 'suitcase committee'; she suddenly has an urgent need to act.

When she emerges from the darkness of the hold, she experiences the first mirage. Her eyes quickly grow used to the sunlit, glittering island again, but there seems to be something else out there now; it is *too* sunny, *too* glittering, so to speak. She stands in the cargo hatch, motionless, confused, incapable of doing anything but gripping on to the edge of the fuselage so she doesn't fall, feeling abruptly dizzy. Something glows near the shore. What is that band of light that troubles and blinds her? Is it the sun shining on the sea again? How can the sea give off such a violent, blinding glare? The flickering drops of light that she found soothing before – which transported her to the memory of previous summers for a few minutes – have become a wall of incandescent gold that threatens to scorch her retinas. She raises her hand, but nothing can shield her from the beam of light. She squeezes her eyes shut, and a band of fire throbs beneath her eyelids. A hand helps her to get down from the plane, step by step, as she can no longer see where she's stepping. A voice, speaking in English, calm and kind. She sits down next to it and half opens her eyes. The brightness of the shore is still there, though weaker now. It does not waver, and so she now reasons that it is not coming from the sea. It is dense and reflective; it is the work of man. *It's the food,* whispers the old woman sitting next to her, who hasn't let go of her hand. The trays covered in foil shine on the sand, and the passengers wait for the heat from the sun to slowly defrost farfalle with chicken and pesto and basmati rice with tomato and courgette. The old woman gives Jimena some water, conscious that her dizziness has more to do with the forty minutes spent unloading bags than with the solar agitation. They say hello and shake each other's hands, but do not say their names. Jimena apologizes for finishing the water and the woman, firm and delicate, squashes the bottle down and puts it into a bag. *I'm collecting them up. We humans are unspeakably disgusting.* Four bags full of rubbish attest to the work of this woman with a clear gaze, flowery dress and straw hat, who walks with a stick. *And it's good for me to get some exercise, anyway.*

For her first foray into the jungle, Jimena is accompanied by one of the cabin crew, and while there she also changes into some clean underwear and a more versatile outfit: a vest top and linen trousers. They enter the treeline between two large rocks that rise up out of the sand unexpectedly. They hadn't seen them a few metres back. Beyond the rocks, the line of brush is dense. The whistles and calls of tropical birds can be heard in the distance, along with buzzing, rustling and tapping. Jimena imagines great hornets, bustling rodents, beetles, grasshoppers and centipedes. She has been terrified of centipedes ever since, as a girl, curled up next to her mother for a siesta, she opened her eyes to see a silent needle pierce the hand that embraced her. Her mother's hand did not swell up or grow deformed, but the venom spread like a claret-coloured stain along the back of it. It stung as if from an acid burn, she said. Jimena remembers observing the irritation, waiting for a deformity that never came. It is due to the possibility, ever arbitrary, of the presence of insects that they decide not to advance much further. They urinate in silence, close to each other, without too much embarrassment. The jungle seems to grow quiet when the humans empty their bowels, as if the animal life has sniffed out something new and, as such, dangerous. *In nature, nothing new is innocuous,* Jimena might have said to me, with that phlegmatic, somewhat fastidious, irritating pedagogical tone she employed when she wanted to apply her specialized knowledge to other, perhaps more reputable, areas of learning. It was a trait that was born from a mixture of quick wit and a detachment that was particular to Jimena, a personal disposition which her work in the natural sciences came to underpin, especially as she gained expertise in her field. The professional attributes she cultivated – of alacrity, diligence and, up to a point, insensitivity – all cemented, or rather, now that I think about it, sustained a previous way of being. Yes, Jimena was cold and pragmatic even before she entered a career in the sciences. But fears do not understand professions – especially if these fears materialized during childhood. As she squats among the trees, she keeps thinking about slippery bodies bristling with feelers squirming beneath the sand, bodies which, disturbed and disorientated, might flock to a fresh source of moisture. She tries to finish as quickly as possible, but something appears on the sand. Not moving bodies of chitin, but little black dots; droplets which, as they land on the white sand, acquire the density of oil. She stands and looks towards the sky, expecting to see traces of resin among the branches above her. The flight attendant is hunting for a handkerchief, while Jimena opts to use the knickers she's changed out of to wipe herself, when she notices the liquid on her lips. Her nose is bleeding profusely.

After eating, a heavy drowsiness spreads over them. As dusk falls, impatience and discomfort also rear their heads – the first signs of civilization. Is there any news? The question bubbles up only to return a little further off a few minutes later, like an underground stream whose current only reappears in very slight, inconspicuous depressions in the ground. No movement can be seen in the cabin and the flight attendants are seizing the opportunity to rest a little after hours of organizing the group and securing provisions. There is still no word of any sort of rescue team. A few people get to their feet and wet their faces, but no one actually swims: the sea seems to hide more than it reveals, and the evening light has darkened the swell. Each passenger has their open suitcase beside them, giving the illusion of intimacy, small private sites of personal property. A somewhat deceptive illusion, as it happens, since all the suitcases are practically the same and Jimena feels a little uneasy after observing their corresponding owners, as she realizes she forms part of the semi-rigid black plastic sector. She didn't realize she was so practical. She promises herself she will buy eye-catching luggage from now on, when they get out of here. It hasn't for a moment occurred to her to think that they won't get out of here, has it? If she repeats the question, an old fear, difficult to pronounce, shows its face. She decides to rid herself of it by busying her mind with some sort of task, but it is not easy to find a suitable activity, and so she starts collecting seashells. More shouting. This time, it sounds like a cry for help. It's coming from the jungle. It is two twenty-somethings who look like surfers, wearing Bermuda shorts and hoodies, and running with that unstable slow gait with which we humans negotiate sand. They are yelling something unintelligible, but they break off as they get to the 'suitcase camp'; they need to catch their breath before they can ask:

'Is there a vet here? Is anyone here a vet?'

This time, they head into the jungle via a tongue of water that snakes into the undergrowth. Jimena, feeling a little bit silly, misses the two big rocks from earlier. What if she never sees them again? Vague nostalgias are activated when we discover a location that we will never visit again. She resolves to go and see them the following day.

'If we walk along the banks, we can avoid all the undergrowth and get in there faster.'

And so they head into the thicket via this course of shallow saltwater; the vegetation – trunks, creepers and flowers – covers the sky like a vaulted roof of greens and golds. Dusk is approaching. Flies and dragonflies, appearing like sunlit motes of dust, fly in meticulous perimeters. The lads are leading the group to a wounded dog, which they hadn't wanted to move.

Thomas is carrying the first-aid kit, and Josh, a harness. A third surfer, whose name – or possibly surname – is Denver, they're told is waiting with the dog, a labrador that was clearly overly curious, or overly cheeky. Jimena, there to fulfil the role of the vet, walks behind them, stepping in their footsteps; Josh has advised her not to walk in the water in case there are scorpion-fish. The jungle is gradually acquiring that gloomy, metallic, militaristic hue that green can take on in certain latitudes when the light fails. Jimena senses once again a gradual cessation in the background noise marking their presence, as if the animals were getting ready to sleep or to attack. She tries to recall any advice from some zoology manual that might dissuade a caiman from creeping up on them, but it doesn't seem necessary – she has only to consult with the surfers, well informed on a variety of jungles from their travels around the world. The boys, athletic, charming and polite, treat her like an older sister. Although she is not thrilled about this, it doesn't surprise her, either: before she left the beach, an old woman sprayed her with perfume without asking her permission, and she is now steeped in jasmine, cinnamon and menopause. *Don't thank me, it's a trick – this way, the predators won't smell your blood.* She just hopes that no bumblebees will mistake her for an orchid. Something is rustling in the far-off branches. Something big. Jimena tries to rouse her adrenaline, prick up her ears, broaden her peripheral vision, but these young Australian guys are all very relaxed. Besides, they won't stop talking.

'Billy ran off after something and came back limping, he's got a really nasty wound. You'll see.'

'Ah, OK, it was around here somewhere.'

They cross a patch of ferns, and Denver and a crestfallen Billy appear. They are surrounded by a dozen coconuts, which the young man has been trying to crack open to pass the time. The image startles her and will be the memory that comes to visit her the most in the future: a young man with a blond beard and a dog, perfectly alone in the middle of the jungle, oblivious to precaution and mistrust. Serenity may liberate us from fear, but does it preclude danger? Jimena would love to think so, and this surprises her; previously, she would have placed foresight and caution on a higher pedestal. She puts the coconut they offer her to one side and examines the dog; one of its front legs is broken, but the most vicious wound is on its jaw. It is bleeding and several of its teeth are cracked; it appears to have been hit with a blunt object. The good news is that the skull hasn't fractured.

'It looks like it's been hit with something like a big stone,' she says, and realizes she is speaking in Spanish.

Of course, these lads speak Spanish, too, and use this language to address her the whole way back. The mystery of the stone doesn't affect Josh or Thomas, but it leaves Denver distraught and pensive. Every now and again he mumbles:

'It's sad, it's so sad.'

And as they reach the last of the coconut trees and get back the light, the afternoon and the open sky, the boy lets out a grunt of frustration, and, with tears in his eyes, utterly devastated, wails at his friends:

'Who would do something like that?'

Josh and Thomas deposit Billy on the ground and hug the anguished Denver, who cries with a touching authenticity. It is then that Jimena, who is looking the other way to try and respect a private moment that no one has asked her to respect, comes across the man and the little girl from before. He is sitting on the ground, his back against the trunk of a palm tree, his head tipped back, his nose pointing up towards the crown of the tree, his neck resting in his daughter's hands. The girl sees her and calls her over, waving her hand a little, nervously. The man looks at her with his eyes half closed, his complexion an oily yellow colour.

'Sorry, nosebleed. I hate getting them.'

Jimena hands him a few tissues and the man tosses the bloody Kleenex away, the breeze sending them fluttering slowly along the ground. She thinks of carnations buried in the sand, although the scene makes her feel somewhat squeamish: the sand has the ability to coat any object in a cloud of filth. They hold their breath until the bleeding stops. Then the man tells Jimena that he needs to ask her a favour.

'I promised I'd take my daughter into the trees to go to the toilet, but I need to rest for a bit longer. Would you mind going with her before it gets dark?'

The girl argues a little with her father in a language Jimena doesn't recognise. She has huge eyes with expressive black lashes. But it is an argument as predictable as her sudden shyness, which then abruptly vanishes once she takes Jimena's hand and heads into the forest with her. On the way in they introduce themselves to one another and Jimena, to her surprise, tells Fairuza about the two big rocks concealed at the other end of the beach. What is it with her and those rocks? She blames it on her difficulty with talking to children. They walk for a few metres through dwarf palm trees, until the girl lets go of her hand to go and climb on to some big gnarly roots to avoid the mud and pools of water. The forest here has transformed into a wetland. Jimena warns her about the scorpionfish, which draws a scathing glance from the girl.

'Let's go a bit further in, I don't like weeing on wet ground.'

When walking through an unknown and tortuous landscape, our slow progress ends up affecting our perception of time. The minutes seem to advance with the same difficulty and indecision with which we take our own tentative, uncertain steps. Perhaps this is why night fell all around them in such a sudden way. The girl was crouching down behind a fallen mossy trunk, finishing up what she had to do, when they heard the shrieks. They came from high up and they were frantic and numerous; it seemed to Jimena that it was the treetops themselves screaming at them to get out of there. Fairuza leapt up and hid behind her, and all Jimena could do, frozen in fear, was to try and count the voices. But they were uncountable. They were deep and loud and desperate. And the shrieking seemed without end – short, rhythmic cries, mixed in with a harsh, unpleasant panting, as if the ferocity of their own wailing had exhausted them. Where could they be coming from? From the land or from the sky? Jimena had no idea to which otherworldly entity they belonged – she couldn't imagine that they were any kind of animal familiar to her.

As if it could tell what she was thinking, a voice behind her, calm and familiar, remarked in English:

'They're chimpanzees.'

It was the old woman who had helped her out of the hold. She was staring into the dark glade, coolly but resolutely gripping her walking stick.

'What do you mean, they're chimpanzees?'

'We should go. Come on, slowly now, my child, you go first.'

Jimena took a step, so frightened and defenceless in the face of the overwhelming bestial presence that by *child* she thought the older woman was referring to her. They walked in silence, very gradually and very slowly, until the shrieks, which did not at any moment let up, were gradually left behind.

'We should really walk through the water – that way we get rid of our tracks. I saw it in a nature documentary on TV back home. I watch a lot of documentaries. Chimpanzees that live in areas without much of a human presence are very violent, far more aggressive than the good-natured image we have of them. They alerted us because they didn't plan on attacking us, I would imagine, but the truth is they could have made mincemeat of us without us even realizing.'

The old woman thought it opportune to end her speech with a soft little chuckle. She was at the head of their small group, beating back the undergrowth with precise swipes of her walking stick, as if she had spent her whole life doing this. It almost seemed as if she were punctuating each pause in the conversation with one of these sharp gestures, which the leaves and stalks did not dare to contradict. She was forceful, but her actions remained elegant and controlled, and they struck Jimena as admirable. Once they had left the swamp behind, she decided to carry the little girl, who had lost a sandal, on her shoulders. And so the party progressed as the sky became stained with sprays of orange and purple. When they finally stepped back on to the sand, the little girl ran off to look for her father. The only thing separating them from the beach was a line of trees, mere black shadows against the dim backdrop of the sea. It was then, once dusk had settled over things, and the colours and the shapes of the world around her had become subdued, that Jimena experienced the second hallucination. They appeared to be fireflies. Little green lights suspended in the air, filling the entire bay. A floating swarm of lights, blinking, at times motionless and close to the ground, at others snaking through the air at shoulder height. Hundreds of fireflies, some moving with a constant rhythm, others circulating slowly until they came to a halt. It was a strange dance, and Jimena thought of will-o'-the-wisps. The old woman kept walking at her side, trampling the ground with her stick and looking down, caught up in trying not to trip over a root, entirely oblivious. Jimena, meanwhile, unable to detect the shadow of the plane or any of her companions, felt vertigo slither along her spine. She was weighing up whether to hide behind a tree trunk when she heard voices. Someone was laughing. She also heard some tinny music. Now she could make out some faces. Blue and green faces, yellow and white faces. Fairuza came running over, holding her father's hand.

'We've got a signal!'

After a long siesta, someone had decided to switch on their tablet to play some puzzle or platform game and within ten minutes had started receiving messages about missed calls as well as notifications from apps and social media. Not only did they have a signal, but their data was working fine, and all the passengers were now doing video calls with their friends and families.

'The geolocation isn't quite working so we still don't know exactly which island we're on,' explained Arash, as Fairuza waved to her mother and grandmother, sitting on the sofa in their house.

'No – it's because we're in a military zone, that's why Google Maps isn't working,' said a boy walking past.

'But have you managed to contact anyone? The embassy, or the airline?' Jimena tried to get her bearings in the torrent of information swirling around her, while simultaneously trying to figure out where the old woman, whom she had lost sight of, was.

'Ah, no, but – didn't you hear? The communications engineer made contact an hour ago with a US military base a few miles away. It's too late to organize a night-time rescue, but they're going to come for us first thing tomorrow. Everything's been sorted out now.'

*

Jimena looks for her suitcase in the half-light, but she can't find it; the night has warped proportions and perspectives – the plane should be closer and bigger, but it is nothing more than a shadow among other shadows. She stumbles over two bottles of champagne; it appears she has missed the celebrations. She has the confused notion that she is at a music festival, trying to find her group of friends in some dark hangar with strobe lights, shifting distances and bodies all packed together. She finds her case at last thanks to the torch on Fairuza's phone. She then uses her own phone to call her family and send a few messages to a close friend who will, in turn, inform Aitana and me. While she is doing this, she also takes the opportunity to inform the people at the conference via her boss. She is surprised by the time – it is only just seven o'clock. She would otherwise have been arriving in Sydney around now. Shortly after, queues form for the few remaining snacks to be handed out as refreshments. As she walks back towards her suitcase, munching some peanuts, she comes across the old woman again, who is using the newly found signal to chat to a son or a nephew. She says hello, but the old woman doesn't see her, and Jimena resolves to go over again later. She is not particularly given to spontaneous gestures of affection, but she harbours a special fondness for her saviour. She sits down and tries to look up at the stars, but the electronic devices lit up all around her invade the darkness and the sky. (The head flight attendant will later have to orchestrate darkness and bedtime, as if they were children.) She observes two men near her, each watching a film on their laptop. She gets up and walks down to the shore. There she sees the starry firmament and hears the waves out on the sea. A doubt comes over her and she is about to look at her phone to check if there are scorpionfish in the Indian Ocean but decides against it, trying to prolong this moment of respite a little longer. She sees a cigarette pulsing in the darkness. A man approaches her; he is nothing but a dark face. They greet each other.

'You know what bothers me? We've hardly left the beach. We're on a desert island and we haven't left this five-hundred-metre perimeter. A desert island and we haven't even explored it! I tried to walk along the shoreline to get to the other part of the coast – I thought maybe there'd be a fishing village, and we were just sitting here in the sun like idiots – but they wouldn't let me. They said that if the rescue mission came and I was nowhere to be found, we wouldn't be able to leave. I get it. I do, really, I get it, but I never imagined that crash landing on a desert island would make me feel so claustrophobic.'

Jimena is tempted to tell him about the injured dog and the chimpanzees, but the man is already proposing they sneak off at midnight.

'Shall we try it? Eh? Shall we go for a walk? Just over to that headland, to see what's there. Or we could go tomorrow morning, first thing?'

'No, thank you.'

'No one wants to come with me.' The man falls silent, staring out at the blackness of the sea.

Back by her suitcase she feels by now as if she is in a small single-occupancy apartment. She has laid a sarong out on the sand and a pair of neatly lined-up trainers greet her. She has had more precarious homes than this. She leaves her sandals by the other pair of shoes, as if staking out the entrance to her cubicle, and prepares herself for the inevitable chill to come. That night she sees more people with nosebleeds. Later, a doctor will inform them that this is completely normal, a result of all the jolting during the accident plus the abrupt change in pressure. They sleep out in the open, some with their backs to the jungle, others with their backs to the sea. (She will soon confess to me, laughing a little sheepishly, that the next thing she knew, and she doesn't really know how – *I promise you I don't know how* – she had her computer open on her lap and was revising the lecture for the following day. She even went as far as opening her emails, but closed the application again quickly and switched off the laptop. She found the book she had been reading and gradually began to drift off. She would have liked it if the shrieks had returned, if the passengers had leapt up in fright and only she, Fairuza and the old woman had been able to calm them down, but the sound of the waves was the only thing she heard during the night.)

It was practically daylight by five in the morning, although the sun had not yet risen. That was when the rushing and a little stumbling around began: they'd been told they could only take one piece of luggage with them, and they had to be ready in half an hour. Jimena gathered her things up quickly and headed over to the treeline they'd visited yesterday to do her business; no sooner had she moved away from the camp than she heard the voices of the flight attendants insisting that everyone come back immediately: the frigate was on its way. Time had inexplicably sped up. She squatted down behind a tree trunk to empty her bowels and, this task completed, indifferent to the gazes of the authorities in this improvised yet efficient civilization, thought about running off to say goodbye to the place she had grown so unexpectedly fond of. She stood there in silence, looking around for the path towards her rocks, and noticed her legs were tense, the muscles ready to sprint. It was as if she were waking from a long dream. Suddenly, her longing to see the rocks seemed childish to her, and so she walked calmly back to the camp. And, unlike the experience by the sea from the day before, she did not feel defeated by some inner force, but rather, secure, confident, fortified.

As she sets off on this final walk back, a crystal-clear conviction accompanies her: she has been lost, confused and mistaken ever since they had the accident, and this is the first correct decision she has taken. What do those rocks matter, in the end? If she goes over the events of the previous day, she does not like herself; she has acted clumsily, she doesn't usually behave like that. She is not surprised to regain a sense of control at this juncture; it confirms for her that she had simply been frightened for the whole of yesterday, that she had felt out of place and unable to think clearly. It is then that sadness and a feeling of profound fragility appear, both of which have been lying in wait, and Jimena will be unsettled by how both feelings had managed to go unnoticed. Sadness and fragility arrive hand in hand. Yes, she had been having a terrible time, she just hadn't realized it until now. If she keeps going, if she studies this sadness, she is sure to discover other hidden feelings, and she decides not to leave this inspection for later, convinced, for better or worse, that the healing process requires a certain amount of willpower. She can detect something close to wounded pride, a general sense of incompetence and imprecision to which she is not accustomed. This may remind her of remote emotions, perhaps from her childhood, which of course she remains keen to ignore. She has never previously felt fragile in this way. She has the sneaking suspicion, too, that some of the people she crossed paths with on the island were making fun of her. This isn't necessarily true, but something has shaken her up inside, and at last, little by little, she thinks she is starting to get over it. Something has broken, but now she is finding ways to repair it. There will be no more doubts, no more fear, no more delusions. She will overcome this, as she has overcome other hardships at other times. Just what it is she has to overcome she does not yet know, but without realizing it, her own habits are already bringing her closer to victory. Behind her, other passengers are also emerging from their hiding places and toilets, eager to get their lives back.

With astonishing punctuality, the frigate appeared on the horizon at the same moment the sun came up. A few people started clapping, and Jimena joined in. The cadets from the US Army acted rather unceremoniously, bundling them all on to the lifeboats. The rescue mission did not seem to have caught them in a very good mood and there was no small amount of shoving and shouting to get people to move quickly. Someone remarked that it was due to the vagaries and complexities of the tides, but the truth is they were shocked by this brusqueness and had the impression they had ceased to be passengers and were instead now hostages or – even worse – refugees. Jimena did not overly care; she was tired of most of the passengers, of their complaints and demands. Discipline was, in the end, a great equalizer.

Just before setting off in the boat, this faux adventure gifted Jimena a fresh anxiety. Along with another twenty people, she was waiting in the penultimate vessel which, for some reason, was not receiving the order to leave. They saw the only male flight attendant scuttle nervously over to the plane; after ten minutes or so, he appeared in the door of the aircraft and shook his head. The head flight attendant went down to the shore to speak with their colleague. They opened a folder and counted the passengers. Apparently, there was one person missing. Jimena looked towards the jungle – probably for the last time – and recalled the older Australian man with whom she had spoken during the flight, and whom she had completely forgotten and hadn't seen since. Would he have tried to explore the island? Might he have failed to return? Where could he be? She fixed her gaze on the silent coconut trees with as much concentration as she could muster, in case a human figure appeared. Or perhaps the man who had accosted her the previous night had decided to head deep into the dense and unknown rainforest. The leaves of the coconut trees waved in the breeze, while the beach displayed the abandoned bags and belongings from their brief encampment. The head flight attendant was talking on the phone. It was all OK. The other attendants confirmed that the missing person was now on the boat. The island was left behind. We could say that there were still a few surprises left to come, but they were quickly resolved and passed off as normal. Certain nuisances and impositions, too, dissipated or even came to be viewed as justified by all these worn-out people. When they arrived at the military base, they were greeted by metre after metre of barbed-wire fencing and were ordered to remove their phone batteries. On the way to the barracks, a bespectacled old man's phone rang and was immediately confiscated. But once there, they were able to shower and eat breakfast, again with some urgency, because there were a few light aircraft waiting for them on the runway to transport them to the Maldives, where a passenger plane would take them to Sydney. At breakfast, Jimena finally managed to say goodbye to the old woman and they shook each other's hands most courteously; she said goodbye to Fairuza and her father, too, and the little girl put down the juice she was drinking to give Jimena a hug. Jimena admits to having felt a slight dizziness when, at seven o'clock in the evening on the fifth of September, she landed in Sydney airport and read her name printed on a sign. The driver, most likely distracted, took her straight to the conference without stopping by the hotel, while the feeling of temporal vertigo tried once more to overpower Jimena. At the conference reception they figured out what had happened and told her not to worry and to go and rest; they had cancelled her presentation, although, they added, they could find her a slot in the timetable tomorrow, the last day. It was up to her.

'And did you give the lecture in the end?' I asked, surprised and somewhat horrified.

'Of course,' she replied triumphantly, and burst out laughing.

Before hanging up, she told me that after giving her lecture, she had lain, showered and fed, on her hotel bed and done a deep dive on the internet to find out where they had been and what exactly had happened. She said that she had verified exactly where they had crashed. She discovered the name of the island and, what's more, the fact that it was not in fact an island, but rather an atoll in the shape of a ring. After the first kilometre or so of trees, there was an enormous saltwater coral lagoon, and none of them had seen it. On a subsequent call, she will tell me the name of the archipelago too, and that the military base where they were taken is a stopping-off point on the way to Guantanamo* and so it was itself probably a US Army detention and torture centre. Prepared to trawl through all her experiences with the utmost diligence and to correct some of her memories, she will also tell me that these islands were originally inhabited but that the British government, in

* Guantanamo Bay Detention Camp was an American maximum-security military prison, located in the far south-east of Cuba, known for its alleged tortures, human rights violations and unlawful trials from 2001 onwards in relation to the invasion of Afghanistan.

cooperation with the US Army, had deported the indigenous population in order to establish a military complex towards the end of the '60s of the last century. At that time, the Republic of Mauritius still claimed ownership of the archipelago. I asked her then if she had solved all the island's mysteries, and, after thinking about it for a second or two, trying to gauge whether my question was well-meaning, she replied that the only thing left to figure out was who or what had attacked the dog. She didn't plan on telling me, but trusted that my powers of deduction would solve this final enigma. *You're perfectly capable of figuring it out, Carlos,* she said, and gave another laugh. Jimena was back to her old ways, determined not to leave any loose ends, nor anything to the imagination.

Years later, however, the island returned to her – the only way, incidentally, that it could return. At the time, both she and I, in our respective worlds, had more or less forgotten the whole incident and each of us was preoccupied with more urgent delicate (not to mention sorrowful) matters. I confess I found the manner in which Jimena spoke to me about it a little strange: it was offhand, as if simply mentioning the island invoked a vanished world. As I listened to a voice note she had sent me about her mother's illness – by then Aitana and I had left, and our conversations could only take place via this channel – she told me about a recent dream.

'At first, I didn't know where I was, although I was sure that I knew the place – that I'd been there before. I was walking along a beach, but there was no one else there, no one at all, and you couldn't hear the waves either, only the constant blowing of the wind. Suddenly I remembered that the aeroplane had to be there, the remains of its wreckage, but there wasn't a single trace of it, not a single wing fragment or a tyre, and no belongings, not one human object, not even one of those little plastic water bottles. I walked towards the forest. Then I tried to look for my rocks and I found them but, as always happens in dreams, they were different, they'd changed. But I knew that they were the same rocks and I touched them, I stroked their surface with my hand. I kept on walking, and beyond the rocks there were no palms, nor any other kind of trees. There was no water, no vegetation, no animals of any kind, only sand. In the distance, the blue of the sea reappeared. The island was a desert, a great sandy plain with no hills or valleys. The wind was a little annoying, but I didn't mind. And I felt really calm because the sun was pleasant and the place wasn't hiding anything; it was all in plain sight. I was surrounded by myself.'

III

MARS IN BLOOM

I had never been in a place like it, had never seen a landscape like it. We were driving up over the mountain pass and you couldn't yet see the sea off in the distance. I remember saying, 'This is like Mars,' and he nodded with a smile and replied, 'When one of my friends first came he said that there must be sun even under the rocks.' From the way he said it I detected a certain sadness, as if this land – his land – were worth nothing and was doomed always to be poor. We rounded the other side of the hill and I began to make out tiny little flowers among the thistles and esparto grass of the desert and, beaming, I added, 'It is Mars, but with flowers!' and he, at the wheel, looked pleased, incredibly pleased. I sensed once again that I had the power to make him both terribly happy and terribly miserable. This moment was a happy moment, and recognizing this power of mine did not matter to me, because I was in love and we had the sea and all the summer ahead of us.

*

All around me are moving boxes and I keep coming across memories of our life together, while I decide what will stay here and what will come with me. I need to be selective; the luggage we can take with us is very limited, so I must choose only what's essential. It's our last night here and we've almost finished clearing the flat: we've given away furniture, lamps and kitchen gadgets; now stripped of our things, the apartment reminds me of how it was when we first moved to live in this neighbourhood. Carlos would say that the flat is a different one now, that it's changed, but I like to think it's remained the same, no more and no less inhabited by our presence. I prefer to think that for each picture I take down from the wall I am reinstating a bit of space, a bit of air, that I am liberating it.

I go out on to the balcony and see, not my reflection on the other side of the street, but rather the light that floats over the structures that don't want to be seen, hovering over and obscuring the hotel complex, with its porticoed courtyard and its swimming pools, and the government buildings, among which is the mansion where the mayor resides. I can't make out any of this, obscured as it is by the illuminated mist. It's March and the air is cool. When I breathe the night air, I exhale condensation and, for a moment, this seems to want to merge with the pallid haze down in front of me. The city blocks below are equipped with the light blockers that have become fashionable recently and that reflect everything around them. And so all these institutional buildings and luxury residences disappear during the day behind a mirror in which local residents and passers-by see only themselves reflected back at them. When I go out on to the balcony to smoke in the mornings, I can no longer see the mayor's inner garden, with its pergolas, statues and fountains, nor her security staff and state cars moving around. I can no longer see the dome, cornices and mouldings of the historic bank that was later converted into a seven-star hotel. Instead, I see myself, far off, silent and pensive, framed by the balconies and windows of my own building. By day the balcony gives on to us ourselves, and if I raise my hand, my reflected image waves back at me. Power is obscured behind a mirror that reflects our collective image back to us. Power is opaque and reflective all at once, a barrier of light. At night, the mirror is switched off, but it gives off all the light retained during the day: the photons spread out in this white glare I am looking at now, they melt slowly away into the sky. I wonder what the inhabitants can see at night if they look out of their big windows – is it always daytime inside? Can they see us?

It's strange that we've ended up living in the centre of town again, a few streets from the first flat I lived in, back when I was still a student. Over fifteen years have passed, and despite the fact that the city has changed a great deal in appearance, I also feel as if, at heart, it is the same as ever, and this certainty, the certainty that it won't change even if we do not live in it, is helping me leave it. Nothing new is going to happen. I think this selfishly, of course, and also, perhaps, to console myself for not having been able to curtail the inertia that's ended up driving us away. Then again, we aren't the first and nor shall we be the last to leave.

But there's no need to dwell on the here and now. Let's see – what am I looking for, exactly?

The sea appeared in the distance. I looked to one side then the other of the motorway, observing all the greenhouses which, to my surprise, were not made of plastic but rather were covered in a yellowish tarpaulin the colour of the soil, as if the dust had buffeted them for years until they blended in with the ground. The famous plastic deserts of the south were not made entirely of plastic. I recall looking inside the covered walkways as we sped past looking for those migrant workers of which we knew so little, whom none of us knew, but who we had read worked in subhuman conditions. I couldn't see anyone, however; the tents of covered crops were all empty and silent. I had just met Carlos's parents for the first time in the city and we were on our way to visit his grandmother. Are we capable of remembering the first time we visited a place we returned to multiple times? I can recall the journey: the motorway, the landscape of fruit and vegetable farms and the desert and, further on, the sea, in a colour so light and muted, so different to the ocean to which I was accustomed. I can recall all the novelties and surprises of this first visit to the south to meet his family, but I can't quite recall the impression it made on me to walk into his parents' house, that residence Carlos had told me so much about, because it is buried now beneath all the other times I went back there. A foreign place that slowly but surely became my home, a strange and exotic family that slowly but surely became my family. The process by which something strange comes to be one's own is a very peculiar one. When you arrive at the house of the woman you do not yet dare even to name, let alone to imagine as 'your mother-in-law', you find yourself in an unfamiliar space faced with unfamiliar people, but at the same time all of this is augmented by the person you love and their memories. You find yourself pulled into the orbit of a past that doesn't belong to you and you must be careful not to move the furniture around too much, not to displace too many of the objects there; if you pay close attention, you can see how your mere presence starts to transform, in real time, the intimacy of a home limited up until that point to a fixed number of components. It is not quite an adoption, because you haven't lost your own family, but I cannot think of a comparable experience: you are an interloper who is welcomed in. No matter how friendly the eventual family-in-law may be, no one knows where the bathroom is on that first visit. And yet, years later, if the relationship is a good one – and ours was, or it used to be – that bathroom will be as much yours as the one in your own family's house and your hand will find the thing it needs without having to switch on any lights. This process slowly erases all the previous misunderstandings and inaccuracies. Human beings can come to accept the previously inconceivable with surprising swiftness. In the right conditions, the first-person plural can expand without fear and without end. Although I also imagine that, in different circumstances, it may well grow more and more narrow, until in this 'us', there is only room for two people. The two of us.

*

'He didn't use to be like this,' Carlos's mother said to me, finding a quiet moment during one visit. 'He wasn't like this a few years ago, believe me. My children don't notice because they don't live here. Or perhaps they do notice, but they soon forget and just keep saying that their father was always like that. But I started to notice it because it was a very quick change, these things happen quickly. There came a time when he'd grown tired of teaching and of the vice-deanship and tried to go back to his original post at the hospital. He said that he was tired of the hardship and pettiness of the university, that he no longer had the freedom to do anything in his department and that he needed a change of scene. And it occurred to him, I don't really know why, that going back to the general internal medicine ward he had emerged from thirty years ago might constitute some kind of challenge or improvement. Seeing patients! Him, who never liked seeing patients. Did he think that this would constitute a better contribution to society? Perhaps. Or perhaps he considered it a way to atone for some sort of guilt for his time in education – bear in mind that it was the start of the crisis, when so many students had to abandon their studies. From one year to the next, many of his best students disappeared, going back home to their parents. I think he felt a little responsible for or complicit in what had happened. But what was he guilty of? Of belonging to a generation? In that case, I too am guilty, we are all guilty. He found that conditions in the hospital were worse upon his return – what with all the cuts, of course. Clogged-up waiting lists, more than forty patients a day, working on Saturdays, emergency departments filled to bursting with people who arrive any old way from houses in any old state. But he had high hopes: he was going to see his colleagues again, his friends from university, who had started work at the same time as him. This hopeful feeling did not last long, however. Meeting up with a lifelong friend to watch the football or celebrate a birthday is not the same as working side by side with that person. "They've got so old," he would say to me. Honestly, I didn't know what to reply. He'd gone searching for the energy of youth in a place where time had stood still, while also passing in a flash. A bad combination. Decrepit twenty-somethings. The many Dr Martínezes, respectable, with their landowner's authority, their airs and graces: Carlos thought that the contemptuous, obstinate, condescending way their teachers had behaved would have disappeared after the dictatorship, but was instead horrified to see that his colleagues had, in turn, morphed into these moustachioed gods in white coats, mediocre and tyrannical. Not to mention the lack of professionalism, having refused to refresh their skills or do any further training after receiving their longed-for qualification. Not to mention the game of seduction and spurning they engaged in with the female nursing assistants. "I went looking for the future in the past. How did I manage to sequester myself away like this? This really is an abduction from the Seraglio," he would say, trying to make a kind of joke out of it, sitting in his underpants on the edge of the bed, not long home from work and still without having had lunch, at four o'clock in the afternoon. Surrounding yourself with old people makes you old, because before, he was surrounded by his students, by his research projects. And what's more, this change of rhythm, this renewed professional intensity on the wrong side of fifty really wears you out physically, and this increased the demoralization that plagued him, a feeling magnified by a general national lethargy. He was trying to hide his exhaustion because I think it made him ashamed. I was still working – and still do now – at a centre for drug addicts that I had worked at since it was set up in the mid-80s, and I was used to the daily rhythm of consultations that was now crushing him. And so he was ashamed, ashamed that, as a man, he wasn't able to cope with the same kind of working day that I had endured day in, day out, fatigued and fed up to the back teeth, but without breaking, without giving in. He was ashamed of the privilege he had enjoyed for all those decades at the university; that the university was demanding I do not doubt, but it was not demanding like this. The demands of pain and illness, the demands of not being able to get up from your chair for eight hours even to have a piss or get a coffee. He began to go and see his mother more and more frequently, to go back to the village he was from, to the sea. He began to sketch out hitherto unheard-of plans, which, moreover, he viewed as always having existed between us. This was what worried me the most. Not that he suddenly wanted to live near the sea, that he wanted to take early retirement and live in a village where we knew no one but his mother – something, incidentally, which didn't interest me in the slightest – but that he was convinced that this was a plan we had spent years talking about together. Because it wasn't that he cultivated this plan in secret, it's that this plan simply did not exist when he was content, happy and stimulated at the university. I think even his mother started to worry, no matter how gratified she was by the increased visits from her first-born son. I see this now, now that everything is somewhat beyond repair. Because there were two options at that point: he could either fully accept defeat – and request a leave of absence due to depression until taking early retirement – or he could give in. And what did giving in mean? Getting used to his new life. Getting used to the hospital, getting used to the many Martínez doctors, tolerating them, excusing them, understanding them. Giving in turns you into a different person. But he took that decision. Then Grandma fell ill and we brought her home, and I suppose that that also meant our lives became an extension of the hospital. And so, listen, I haven't discussed it with Carlos – my husband – and I haven't discussed it with Carlos – *your Carlos* – either, but I've set it all up so that when we are elderly we will move into an old people's home. I don't want us to be a burden. I don't want to age you both. Don't ever change your plans, do you hear me? I no longer know the person I married. I've had to try really hard to love him again, do you know what I mean? Keep all your projects going. Don't ever betray yourselves.'

Sometimes, our family-in-law discover in us, the outsiders, a confidante, or perhaps merely a witness (we don't, it seems to me, ever quite reach the status of a confessor). They tell us things about their inner lives they would never tell their children. We are suitably distant, if you like, and appear in their lives with the right level of maturity. I don't know, I'm just thinking about it now, but we must be an appealing, wished-for presence. A trusted stranger is the ideal person to help you come to terms with your family, with the image your family have of you. What was unexpected and slightly daunting to me was that my in-laws took so little time to lay themselves bare, to open themselves up. I must have had this conversation with Carlos's mother the third or fourth time I was with her, perhaps the first time we were on our own, both knowing that we wouldn't be interrupted, and I had the feeling, young as I was, that it was the first time an adult was talking to me. Now, on this night of farewells, I wonder if it was the first time she had told anyone what she was telling me. That is, whether I, similarly, was the first adult she had been able to talk to.

Perhaps my mistake was not breaking anything. Perhaps we should have broken something so as to have a better idea of what we were made of.

We parked the car and walked to his grandmother's apartment. She still lived in the little town on the coast at the time of that first visit. A 'little town on the coast' which, to my surprise, had 40,000 inhabitants. And so the Mediterranean showed me its most productive side: the remote fishing village I had imagined in fact turned out to be an unceasing screen of apartments along the length of a vast seafront promenade, and then, further inland, the neighbourhoods where the hospitality staff and greenhouse workers stayed. Carlos seemed to be apologizing for the view, but I didn't mind, I was thrilled by the bustle of people and businesses and the rough-and-ready holidaymaking, which I had never witnessed, where the local resident and the tourist are practically indistinguishable. Where I am from, holidaymaking was the preserve of distinguished people, or those from Madrid with compound surnames, subjects perfectly *distinguishable* from the rest of us, if you'll forgive my wordplay. This kind of holidaymaking was something else; everyone seemed to be in on it. But I didn't notice the devastation, either. I couldn't tell that behind this housing development a hill had disappeared, or that the bay I was looking at had been carved up to construct a second marina and two nightclubs which had, of course, already gone bankrupt and closed down. Then again, how can one think back to how any given landscape looked prior to any construction work taking place there? What details or contours in the land would allow us to recognize what it once was? Could Carlos or any member of his family really even recall what the 'nothing' prior to this 'everything' was like? Could they bring to mind something as indeterminate as a mountain? It is very hard to retrieve disappeared spaces in one's mind – it is always a strained attempt at displacement: removing this assemblage of semi-detached houses, substituting for it something that is no longer there. An exercise doomed to failure, since one must do it afresh daily and struggle with the persistent, stubborn presence of the material. And I suppose that we survive precisely because, sooner or later, we give up viewing everything with the eyes of the past. This family, however – especially Carlos's father and older brother – went on and on about what had been destroyed, as if something had been taken away from them. And I don't doubt that they *had* lost something, but I never found out what, exactly.

Behind the window dressing of the towering apartment blocks, the houses were humbler and spoke of the area's mining and fishing past. And it was here that generosity and good cheer could be found. It was vivid and touching. There was no business where I wasn't gifted some small trinket, no bar where we weren't bought a drink or two. 'They give you more freebies, but they also rob from you more,' one of Carlos's teenage cousins said to me during a trip to the beach. In his grandmother's apartment I was met with this same combination of delight, intimacy and simplicity: a table covered in plates and bowls with chips, cockles, mussels, olives, cheese, serrano ham, a blood sausage with onion and a spicy blood sausage (two different types of blood sausage!), dried fruit, little savoury empanadas, and several products typical of the local area – a paprika tart with a dried sardine on top, for instance – which were a marvel of humility and character, and summed up, from my enthusiastic point of view, everything I had seen up to then: the sun, the desert and the sea. Next to all this, instead of salad, there was some chopped cucumber sprinkled with salt, but no oil. 'What do you mean there's no salad? Do you want it now? I was going to bring it out with the main meal, this is just to start.' And so after all this, we ate salad, paella, fruit and ice cream. That same night we went out for dinner locally so that the experience of being with his family wouldn't be too full-on (the cousin I mentioned earlier and an aunt of Carlos were both in the apartment with us), and when we came back, we were met by his grandmother waiting for us with a second dinner. 'Lord only knows what you'll have eaten out there, *Nene*.'

For some people, remembering means putting images together, but I think to remember is to refresh our emotions. I didn't visit this town enough times for it to become an internalized landscape, I wasn't there frequently enough, perhaps, for each trip not to be merely a renewal of the previous one, a renewal of still-novel sensations. Each time was a little like the first time; we must have only visited three or four times before his grandmother fell ill and moved to live with his parents in the capital, and the apartment, in the end, was sold. I don't know if when we fall ill we become different people to those we used to be, but what I am convinced of is that, despite their lives routinely ending with an image of decline, we take pains to remember our loved ones as independent of their illness. When I recall Carlos's grandmother, it is always the same person who appears by my side. I remember that I had never met such a cheerful, jolly old woman; she had such a mischievous sense of humour and a remarkable ability to turn everything into a joke – even mass, which she attended like clockwork. This was why her belligerent outbursts surprised me: they didn't seem to be part of her; they formed a version of her that was unknown and remote.

When siesta time came around everyone went to their rooms, and I stayed sitting with Carlos's cousin playing video games. We were playing a shooter – *Medal of Honor: International Brigades* – when his grandma woke up and brought us some iced coffee. I saw Carlos's cousin grow tense and try to pause the game, but there was a water tank about to fall on us, and a Red Cross truck full of schoolchildren waiting on the other side of the square. Grandma put her glasses on and stared at the screen. 'Already shooting people, eh? Who are you shooting at?' 'They're Nazis, Grandma, we're rescuing children.' When she realized that we were members of the International Brigades shooting at soldiers from Franco's army and the Third Reich, while concluding a fictitious evacuation of Guernica, she flushed red with anger and walked out of the little living room where we were playing without saying a word. 'We're saving the children, Grandma,' my commanding officer added as she closed the door. I heard voices in the hallway; she was arguing with Carlos, who wasn't one to avoid thorny topics. I heard references to 'murderers' and 'communists', and Carlos replying, 'Worse than Mussolini.' She shot back with an unexpected 'Negrín.' Then she burst back into the living room and we hit pause – for real this time – on the game. 'You kids think you're so smart,' she said, looking at me. 'You think you know everything. You do – you think you know everything. And you know nothing. Nothing at all.' She walked out again, and Carlos followed her into the kitchen to try and talk to her some more, and soon they were back to laughing. His cousin shrugged and told me not to worry. With his blond hair and grey eyes, exotic for this unequivocally southern family, he really did look like a British member of the International Brigades.

Over the years, Carlos's grandmother's words have acquired new meanings, all of them pretty dismal. A shiver runs down my spine when I recall them, as if at heart, buried somewhere deep within her, this old woman, who was six when the Civil War started, knew something that we had no inkling of. It is late and I've got half the lights on in this uninhabited apartment. I walk around and switch them off, one by one, as I wrap a woollen shawl around myself, which I decide I'll later add to the suitcase to come with me. Carlos is still asleep in what is left of our bedroom, his breathing laboured. When he sleeps, he always seems worried; when he is awake, however, he is always, or almost always, in a good mood. I take a seat on the floor, near the big window. Now that I only have a reading lamp on, I notice that this new urban glow, motionless and white, is quite similar to the light of the full moon. It seems as if from now on, there will be a full moon every night in this city.

'She didn't use to be like that,' Carlos said when we got into the car to continue our journey. It felt as if everyone in his family had changed, or no one quite matched up to everyone else's memories of them. We carried on heading southwards, towards the desert, to a nature reserve where we were going to camp for a few days. Naked and lazy, on our return from this lunar landscape, our skin would react with suspicion to our clothes and shoes, having forgotten about the cold temperatures and the city air. We were, for a few days, blissfully uncivilized. The austerity of the landscape was set against aquatic abundance. We spent the day swimming and diving among shoals of silvery fish, electric shocks of underwater life, currents of blue above a sandy seabed in perpetual motion, one that hid sole, crabs and small squid. Nothing was still. Refracted sunlight mixed with the presence of hundreds of bright needles and the sea floor churned with the swaying of the Neptune grass. Unaccustomed to and confused by so many reverberations, I steadied myself against a submerged rock, keen for some promise of stability; I surfaced to take a breath and, before I knew it, my feet were surrounded by specks of blue and lemon, golden leaves, friendly little cartoon fish with green and orange fins, which waved and nuzzled with a mixture of fear and respect. Eventually I would understand that the only stillness to be found was in the depths of the oceanic darkness, a truly neutral horizon, and so I resolved to surrender and let myself drift. I would return to land exhausted and rested all at once. Each time we would venture a little further, each time we would reach more remote coves. We would drive down goat tracks in Carlos's father's old car, a burly, oversized Volkswagen, and I would sift through the cassette tapes in it. The soundtrack to Carlos's childhood. I would put something on and then quickly stop it because it depressed me; this family took pleasure in listening to gloomy singer-songwriters, to sad, contemplative melancholies. This is what it meant to be well-to-do; this was what the Spanish middle-class listened to. I belonged to a different class, and these details made me realize that my family did not permit the luxury of indulging in sadness. Sadness, even in a recording, is never inoffensive. I looked often at the map on my phone, the landscape reduced to its most minimal expression: rocks and sky, ochre and blue. The sun bore down on everything, and only in the afternoon did the hills show their reds, mauves and violets. Every cove, every bit of rock, every minute fluctuation in the landscape had been named, at times in ways that seemed quite makeshift, coined out of the day-to-day necessities of fishing and shepherding from centuries gone by: Punta Chica, Punta Negra, Punta Redonda, Punta Molina, Cala Amarilla, Cala Blanca, Cala de las Mujeres, Cala de los Lucas, Cerro Gordo, El Cerrillo, Cerro Seco, Cerro Berruezo. That day, we spent over an hour deep in that rocky landscape and didn't see another soul. The map on my phone stopped giving the names of peaks, paths and hills: we were in a remote, inaccessible, dusty place, one that was entirely anonymous. When I pointed this out to Carlos (he always drove; the thought of doing so made me feel half lazy, half apprehensive), he replied that he found this comforting – it meant that we were far away from everything. And I tried to feel this same lightness, induced by being in spaces that have not been named.

The idea of having children scared him, because he associated it with the definitive loss of childhood. And yet, sooner or later, he would lose his childhood, with or without children. Over time, just as I had imagined, it dawned on him that his childhood memories – the endless, carefree summers – had ceased to be a haven and had become instead an encumbrance. The world of the past was growing older around us, and the attachment to certain panoramas that were now disintegrating could only lead to his own disintegration: childhood had become an inexorable source of vulnerability. He then remembered that having children is the fastest way to kill off one's own childhood. And this enterprise, the only one that could free him from the past, soon became a matter of urgency. But I had no interest in it, though I had always imagined myself as a young mother. Perhaps because at that point, when he suggested it to me, I had just turned thirty. I have come to the conclusion that one can only have children either very early or very late; in the intervening period, life is too unique, too fun and too boundless. How can you choose to limit, to curb something you have been waiting for your whole life to open up?

And what's more, was Carlos not like a child to me? Did I not have to be careful so as not to hurt him? I remember that, when I started going out with him, in our last year of university, I was surprised by his fragility. And not because I wasn't accustomed to male fragility – my father was a bundle of kindness and angst – but rather because it was so unexpected. Suddenly he was the sensitive one, the nervous one, the one with all the worries, but also the hopeful one, the helpful one, the tender one, the affectionate one. Was I not all those things as well? Were we not very similar, the two of us? So emotional, so empathic that we found other people's pain too much to bear. He enjoyed the cachet of these attributes, because in him they were a reason to be proud and stand out, while in my case they constituted a facet society took for granted in a woman, and as such were not even discernible. If we were so alike, was I in that case a child to him, too? Could it have been another way?

As a couple, we had become the parents in a nuclear family comprised of our friends – that married pair who take you in, comfort you and feed you, adoptive parents for all those people who couldn't get over their worries in the bosom of their own family. After all, in Madrid no one is from Madrid and people's families are far away, which forces you to form – and to choose – a new family. We were also the only couple in our circle that did not break up in those years of economic collapse – the upheaval provoked by the mass exodus of our generation also had a cost in terms of romantic relationships.

Carlos and I were sponges; we soaked up each other's happiness and sadness. On the day we moved from our attic room to a bigger apartment, he was enthusiastic and cheerful and I a little downcast at leaving our first home; he, seeing me so unhappy, saw everything we were leaving behind through my eyes and grew equally stricken and distraught. And I got over my sadness when I saw him so suddenly crestfallen, and so realized that it wasn't such a big deal. It wasn't that he appropriated my sadness so he could embody it in himself, it was a reciprocal mechanism. I don't mean that he took control of everything. I would also worry about *his* worries and he, in turn, would worry when he realized that I was worrying about something of his, and in this way we would both enter into a prolonged cycle of upset that, to a certain extent, ashamed us. We were ashamed to be so sensitive.

I'm only giving examples of unhealthy emotions here, though. Does one soak up anxiety faster than happiness? No, absolutely not; it's this evening that's so long and so uncertain that's making me see things that way; we were also capable of cheering each other up in a flash.

But the question remains: is he weaker than me? Did I need to be so cautious through all our years living together, taking care not to wound him? After all, wasn't I supposed to have this majestic, absolute power, this ability to make him 'terribly happy and terribly miserable'? And who had granted me this power? I had. It came from me. No one had asked me to take up this responsibility.

In this next stage of our life together, I will have nothing more to do with his suffering. Because it is eternal and exhausting. Because it is the only way forward that won't drive us apart and leave me feeling guilty.

What is staying here and what is coming with me? I've been focusing on this question all evening. Through it, I'm regaining my energy, and will be leaving here hopeful. But only time will tell if there are ways of understanding this departure that are not through the prism of defeat.

I've read his stories: I know how he views me, how he views himself. It's always been assumed, too, that my views could contain both of us, could bring us together. I'm not sure if spending this last night gathering fragments of our life as a couple was the right thing to do, but it's not *my* life I need to make peace with, it's *our* life. What scares me the most is setting off on such a long and lonely journey with a person who perhaps knows me too well, who perhaps *knows me by heart*. How can I make the opposite journey, how can I make the familiar go back to being something strange again? How can we get to know each other all over again?

And so, I'm not choosing the memories I want to bring, but rather those I wish to leave behind. This is why I'm leaving it all written down, so they no longer form part of me, and so that we can, if not start from scratch, then at least play at discovering each other afresh. Sitting here, I'm left with a collection of texts that are a little gloomy, when I was hoping, somehow, to celebrate our happiness – our past happiness. But it's night-time now and it is terrible to know a person too well and to make the journey we are getting ready to make.

I have always seen snow as a white desert. On the plains of Castile, from the car or the train, when I travelled north to see my family. I hope I can look at this white desert we are about to set off for as a snow-covered landscape. The woollen shawl is coming with me.

IV

FREED SPECTRUM

'Where are you guys? I can't see you. I can't see any of you.'

I didn't say it loudly. Rather, I murmured it. I went around murmuring it like a refrain as I circled the house, passing once more in front of the barbecue, the garden chairs with rush seats, the rose bushes and the planters. The hedge of cypress and cedar, savagely pruned, enshrouding the perimeter of the plot of land in darkness: the December dusk had caught us off guard as we sat around talking after lunch. There was no one there. At the gate, the entrance to the grounds, by the curved slope where the cars were, I thought I could make out a presence behind Diana's Ford. Are we capable of perceiving a body's desire to go unnoticed, to disappear? This is what they call a 'sixth sense', isn't it? The sensation that something is there, despite us not being able to see or hear it. Can we intuit in some way – in a way that doesn't involve the normal perceptual system – that unnatural silence, that held breath, tense and expectant, even though it emits no sound? I walked slowly, my ears spooked, straining to catch any movement of air, any slight tremor from the physical universe that might offer me a clue – or at the very least, a suggestion – as to whether there was a figure crouching there. I write 'physical universe', and perhaps it sounds a little over the top, but in this state of high attention and alert – regardless of whether we're only playing at being alert, we remain alert – we become machines that amplify reality. And so we compel a brain that's somewhat overwhelmed – and maybe a little tired, too – to hear a footstep or heavy breathing in something which perhaps is no more than a leaf in the wind, a raindrop on a window ledge or the creaking of a wall that has struggled to cope with the abrupt changes in temperature. (Incidentally, it was cold during our stay in that mountain villa outside Madrid.) I crouched down, convinced – utterly convinced – that one of my friends was behind the red car with its slightly peeling paintwork, but nope, no one. And just as I realized there was no one there I felt set upon once more by a dozen invisible sets of eyes, a crowd of shadows all around me. Does that not happen to you guys, too? That when you're playing hide-and-seek you spur your senses on so much that you end up interrogating reality until it gives you some sort of sign, some sort of indication of a presence within the silent emptiness that seems to teem and sigh with your old acquaintances, turned all at once into uncomfortable, restless prey? With which part of the body do we feel hidden gazes? I started to feel a tingling on the back of my neck and shoulders. Even if it's no more than a deep, elemental suggestion, the exhalation of a fervid brain, I do not doubt that imagination helps us to survive certain invisible dangers. Or perhaps this intense imagination, which registers non-existent threats and sees things where there are none, emanates from distant instincts that are now pretty much obsolete, since the tangible, rapacious dangers of the wild have been eradicated. I remember that, as a teenager, in the house where we spent summers, a rocky, desert-like landscape all around, I became obsessed with the possibility of thieves getting in. One eternal night, unable to sleep, training my ears on the upper floor (the bedrooms were on the ground floor, protected from the heat), I clearly caught the sound of a footstep in the kitchen, right above me. Just one footstep. I waited for a while, clinging to a baseball bat I kept hidden under my bed, but heard nothing else. Just one footstep. After a few minutes I realized that my system for detecting and interpreting reality had manufactured and re-encoded an arbitrary signal – the gurgling of the motor in the fridge, for example – until it had transfigured it into what my overflowing levels of adrenaline demanded.

The darkness was acquiring a thick quality; I took two steps in the direction of the chalet, imagining that everyone was inside, waiting for me. Who was stalking whom? Hide-and-seek is, to be quite honest, annoying. I've always thought so. I want to believe that all games are a mark of civilization, and, in this specific case, we reinterpret the ruthless, bloody hunts of ancient times, since the present has turned us into predators without a purpose. Unless we're experiencing war. We might, then, regard hide-and-seek as training for a war that has not yet materialized. But no one hunts or wages war alone, and perhaps no one should play hide-and-seek at the age of twenty-eight. Nonetheless, the terrors, fears and adrenaline are all still there, inside us, and this pale, motionless mass which can be made out between the black trunks of the hedge must, without a doubt, belong to someone. I run towards it and hear a sigh and a scuffle, I realise it's Aitana, then I spin around and bound up the steps to the house three at a time, burst into the hallway like a hurricane and smack the table as I bellow out her name. She comes in, slowly. We look at each other. I am panting, red, dripping with sweat, my side hurts; she is covered in dust and cobwebs. She sneezes.

'What's the point of all this when we've brought a whole stack of games with us?'

Javier was inside an old trunk, Irena under a wardrobe, Eduardo in the bath, with a rug on top of him – a frankly conspicuous hiding place. Diana, meanwhile, showed up wrapped in a rolled-up duvet on the floor (she squealed when I stepped on her by accident), and Enrique was curled up in a ball on top of a bunk bed. The only thing left for me was to go down into the semi-basement, which was where the garage, the musty little living room, the dark corridors, the guest bedroom and the boiler all were. The most terrifying surprise of the afternoon – at least until that moment – occurred when I heard noises coming from the aforementioned living room – a confined space filled with old books, a drinks cabinet, sad old toys and paternal trophies – realized that the light didn't work, and sensed, through the gloom, that a sofa was sneezing. I threw a rubber at the sofa (I had decided to come armed), and it let out a little yelp. Then this mass with a canvas cover on it began to shake and wobble like a blancmange, and it seemed to me as if the material was completely disintegrating, like some kind of hideous cartoon, until Eric's head, asphyxiated, appeared from under the cover, at the base of the sofa, and asked me for help. He and Jimena had got stuck in the frame; they literally were the sofa. They had taken the cushions off and dismantled the whole thing, even unscrewing the light bulbs from the ceiling so the room would be in darkness. For reasons we never probed into, they had decided to lie down on their fronts with their legs bent back to form the back of the sofa. I closed the door and left them there in the dark as Sandra, the instigator of this spooky game, scampered around, hopping and shouting as she freed my prisoners from their jail. The only person left to find was Paquito Pacheco, the owner of the house, although he had probably gone off to have a smoke and collect pine cones for the fireplace. It was New Year's Eve 2014, and we had managed to get together after a year without seeing each other.

After shouting out for Pacheco and not getting a reply, Eric, Sandra and I took the keys to his Hyundai – left behind, along with his phone and his wallet – to go and buy food and drink, while Diana and Aitana went off to look for firewood. No sooner had we started the engine than we heard a peculiar noise, a strange sort of purring. We let the car roll down the slope in neutral. Eric, in the back, asked me to turn off the engine. A muffled little voice came from behind the back seats, pleading.

'Help . . .'

We opened up the boot and there, gasping for breath, was Pacheco, his face creased and pale.

'Don't ask me why I did that.'

He limped off back towards his house, winner of the game and victim of his own hiding place. I wouldn't want to put too much emphasis on how much we laughed, because describing other people's laughter is a tedious undertaking, and is generally counterproductive. Let's just say it was a lot.

We tried to cater for all criteria and sensitivities, but this is not always an easy task for a dinner with the commemorative, opulent nature of New Year's Eve, and so the contents of our trolley included, in unstable equilibrium, seafood and pastries, cava and packets of crisps.

'What's the point of buying vegetables and bones to make stock if we can buy ready-made stock in a carton? Look, this one's all right.'

'This one's cheaper.'

Sandra and Eric were not known for their love of celebration or opulence, and I was worried I had selected the most austere, unimaginative members of the group to serve on the committee of gastronomic acquisitions, two people whose chosen lifestyle – if this works as a justification – was practically a form of survivalism.

'Come on, let's have a bit of luxury, Carlos, it is Christmas, after all.' Eric was brandishing half an Iberian sausage, whose label proclaimed it was only '50% Iberian pork'.

Supermercados Sotolix, the go-to supermarket chain in the Cuenca Alta del Manzanares, wasn't exactly making things easy, either, specializing as its stores did in cured meats, criollo chorizo and lamb, as well as a comprehensive range of barbecues and utensils for skewering, smoking and tenderizing.

'Why should we "invest" in langoustines if for the same price we can get a load more hamburgers? Look, these ones look good.'

'No one ever eats prawns, anyway. We'll just say they'd sold out, problem solved.'

I imagined the predictable rage from the Atlantic (Jimena, Aitana) and Mediterranean (Javier, Diana, Eduardo, me) contingents if there was no seafood on the menu, and so I waved the shopping list once more, determined not to let myself be bullied by this waiter who had settled in Berlin or the chemist who had made her home in Frankfurt.

'Maybe we just make spaghetti with tuna and tomato sauce for dinner instead? We can cook five kilos and whatever's left over we can eat the next day,' I argued, and they tried to figure out whether I was insulting them, which, naturally, I was.

We bought white and brown baguettes, industrial loaves of bread, burger buns, tinned tomatoes, whole tomatoes, cured ham and cooked ham, croissants, coffee, decaf coffee, milk, oat milk, lactose-free milk, own-brand chocolate donuts, a few fuet sausages, Eric's premium sausage, criollo chorizos, four dozen eggs, packets of bacon, hamburgers, fresh sausages, pork loin, crisps, nachos, two tubs of hummus, pickled anchovies, appetizers, olives stuffed with anchovies, potatoes for cooking, six tins of tuna, two bottles of mayonnaise, gherkins, capers, three tins of artichokes, escaroles, endives, almonds, dates, white cheese, blue cheese, Camembert, a jar of roasted peppers, two long peppers, onions and garlic, a head of celery, carrots, a leek and a turnip, a pack of cooked prawns, thirty litres of beer, two bottles of gin, a bottle of rum, tonic and various soft drinks, the obligatory grapes, a little box of chocolates and a tiny bottle of Codorníu cava. I managed to abort the purchase of two packets of ham and cheese rolls ('These are tasty and we wouldn't have to cook tomorrow') and the frozen calamari ('I bet these are good, I'm dying to try them, they don't have them in Germany'). Considering there was nothing especially luxurious, memorable or sexy about this haul, beyond a few shellfish which had been frozen and transported from remote waters, we decided to buy a tin of red scorpionfish paté.

'We haven't bought anything different to what you'd buy for a normal weekend in the country! This looks like a stoner's trolley! There's nothing special in it!' I exclaimed in dismay.

'What do you mean? We've got endives!'

'And dates!'

(Fortunately, bottles of wine and bones for making stock were waiting for us at home, along with a special dish – an octopus – all of which had been discreetly transported by Javier in a shared car.)

Sandra danced something she called 'the scorpionfish dance' and we stepped out into a practically empty car park and a still, icy evening that seemed to heighten the outlines of everything, leaving them crisp, immaculate. The stars shone as far as they were able to, penetrating the blanket of light pollution, and the lights around the edge of the reservoir merged and intermingled with the distant residential developments and an immense prison mostly housing those who were caught stealing from public coffers. Eric, unfamiliar with the country's mountainous regions, insisted that all these lights were landing strips. He wanted to see the glow of the international airport down below, to see where most of the group had been deposited, arriving from their lives abroad. On the way back to the house we waved at businesses and facilities closed for the holidays: big hardware stores, bullfighting bars, garden centres with glass-covered nurseries, the sports centre, the pelota court and the bowling alley. We drove along the main road, empty on this, the last evening of the year, and at every roundabout, all the exits fanned out towards residential precincts of great, solid grey stone houses surrounded by sombre black railings, big mansions with some twenty rooms, rigid, solemn, austere and implacable. On each of the roundabouts, a monument to a member of the Civil Guard or a soldier killed by ETA rose up, monoliths in the ubiquitous grey granite. A hole had been drilled towards the top of the statues. We counted nine roundabouts – nine monuments – on our way back.

'Is it an allegory for the bullet in the back of the head?'

'I can't think of another explanation.'

The roofs of black slate only added to the impenetrable image of these residences, and the relentless granite stretched out, uniform, as far as the eye could see, or as far as one's memory of history books went, from la Morcuera to El Escorial by way of Cuelgamuros.* The suburb where Pacheco and his parents had spent all their summers exhibited slightly friendlier dimensions: manageable plots, familiar vegetation and modest, everyday materials; not even in their small two-storey house of brick, Artex and tile, however, was it possible to fully escape the strict visual doctrine of eagles and crucifixes, rocky balustrades, jagged pine groves, and the sharp crests of distant, stormy peaks, fractured by dark ravines. The landscape, whether human or mineral, was organized with an iron-like consistency.

'This is like one of my screenplays,' Javier remarked, when he figured out that none of the TV channels had a signal.

Pacheco, by now recovered, was fiddling with the aerial

---

* La Morcuera Pass can be found in the Guadarrama mountains to the north of Madrid. The monastery and royal residence of San Lorenzo de El Escorial is a vast Renaissance structure that includes a palace and a basilica constructed during the reign of Philip II in the sixteenth century. It includes a royal mausoleum where many of the kings and queens of Spain are buried. The Valle de Cuelgamuros, previously known as the Valley of the Fallen, is a giant monument made up of an underground basilica and a 150-metre-high cross. It was constructed during the dictatorship of General Franco and was one of the most recognizable and persistent symbols of that period. In it are interred 33,833 combatants from the Spanish Civil War, whose remains are fused with the structure of the building. It also contained the tomb of General Franco until his exhumation in 2019. During the extreme right-wing biennium (2032–4), a proposal was raised to return the dictator's remains to the basilica, which proved highly controversial.

cable. As this didn't seem to work, he tried switching the DTT* device off and then on again. Aitana, Javier and I were tidying up the living room to make space for our festive dinner. The main table was cluttered with roads, ramparts and little plastic soldiers, coloured darts and a series of hexagons that made up the map of Catan.

Javier worked for a thirty-something commercial film director who was undergoing a life crisis of some kind. He was therefore attempting to get some films off the ground that marked a return to the site of his childhood dreams and adolescent ambitions, that returned to what he called 'the *original form*', to everything that had motivated him to devote his professional life to the conventions and mechanisms of motion pictures in the first place. He was a man splashing around in hundreds of thousands of euros earned from adverts for cars and beer. Javier, who had been at the state film school with him, had been brought in as a screenwriter, in deference to youthful schemes and illusions, and was responsible for bringing this fantasy of his old project partner to life. The director, a carefree kind of person with a fast-paced love life, who lived in a penthouse apartment awash with psychedelic rock memorabilia, baseball caps, arcade machines and little models from inter-galactic wars, was offering him the perfect

---

* Digital terrestrial television. A technology that operated through the binary encryption of sounds and images emitted by terrestrial electromagnetic signal. It was introduced in 2010 in Spain, and required a specific decoder.

route back to the adventures of old: esoteric mysteries on a desert island, psychological suspense on a space station, eerie assaults on an isolated family, rustic chases where sophisticated technology is coupled with the physical rigours of animal survival. A series of shipwrecks, in essence, set in near futures and with one common backdrop: the end of the world. In all these fictions, sketched out in the thick tobacco-filled air of the director's office, was the promise of the collapse of civilization – it was the ultimate threat, and it always appeared. The possibility of collective catastrophe was the starting point for an anomalous, disturbing situation, and it fell to the protagonists to discover whether this breakdown was real or fake: if everything really was coming to an end and they would have to stake their chances on escape, resistance or sacrifice, or if, conversely, this apocalypse was in fact the illusion of a paranoid digital society, obeying the interests of a series of shadowy corporations in order to control the world's population. Of course, another option was that it all formed part of a deranged father's plan to lock up and tyrannize his wife and children.

'I want us to write a 100-minute-long episode of *Lost*,'* said this director, and Javier shook his hand over the pool table that

---

* *Lost* was a six-season series created by Jeffrey Lieber, Damon Lindelof and J. J. Abrams for the ABC channel, and originally broadcast between 2004 and 2010. The show, which narrates the adventures of the passengers of a flight that crashed on an island that was seemingly deserted, but which in reality was enshrouded in mystery, was a global phenomenon.

occupied much of the living room in his penthouse, reigning over the toys and figurines from legend. The room was a heterosexual male paradise which sooner rather than later would implode into alcoholism and a premature divorce.

Javier was chewing gum and slotting the plastic soldiers into their little stands while chatting about these adventures in storytelling:

'One of the main issues we have in the stories we're writing is that the plots are always based on the absence of information. Intrigue, by definition, is based on concealment. All suspense is constructed on doubt, on the idea that the characters don't know exactly what is happening. They know something, but they can't consider what's happening in its entirety. They don't know for certain if these strange glowing lights, which the couple in crisis observe at night from the remote country house where they've retreated to rekindle their love, are startling but harmless atmospheric phenomena or . . . air strikes from biological warfare, as the peculiar forest warden who has knocked at their door claims. But all the ambiguity of a situation falls away the moment we can phone somebody or check the news. And so, at the start of every screenplay, we've always got this complicated moment when we have to isolate the protagonists. It's a dramatic manoeuvre that the viewer tends to see as artificial. Forced. Perhaps clichéd. Think about it: in recent horror films, the characters always lose contact early on, there's always a sequence, increasingly laboured, where in the middle of the woods someone says, 'How strange, I can't get a signal!' Reliable connectivity, stable twenty-four hours a day, interferes with any kind of suspense. We've tried it, we've tried to write apocalyptic thrillers set in the present day where there's no lapse in the flow of information, but it's hard, it's really hard, as if the sub-genre itself won't allow it.'

'What about a period piece? Like some strange visitors showing up in the Civil War, or the Napoleonic Wars?'

'We can't invoke the same anxieties in a Carlist war* as when we present them in a world similar to our own, headed for destruction. Not if you want to make something in the apocalyptic genre, I mean, something commercial. I'd love to see an alien film set during the conquest of the Americas, but Marcos wants something with story, something conventional, pacy – he doesn't want the viewer to leave a single crumb of popcorn in the tub. So, the fears have to be contemporary ones. And fear in turn is fuelled by ignorance, by lack of communication. In order to cut the characters off, in a way that's convenient but not too explicit, we have to distance ourselves a little more each time: taking them to truly remote places, or sending them into some desolate science fiction, like an astronaut abandoned on a satellite or a moonbase. We can adapt the Western to extraterrestrial lands, but not too much – we can't lose that connection to the social angst of today, we have to acknowledge the system of desires and suspicions that surrounds the characters. It's important that the present is

* The Carlist Wars took place in Spain between 1833 and 1876. They were a series of civil wars related to the line of succession and the conflict between different monarchical, traditionalist or liberal political factions.

projected on to the future. As Marcos keeps saying: "We can't go beyond 2030, no one will believe us."'

'Can someone take over here? I've got to go and take a look at the fire.' Pacheco was changing channels with the remote, but the TV remained dark.

'We've got no connection. It's official, we're in one of my films now. First we'll joke about it, then someone will turn up, an old woman or a soldier, to warn us that we can't leave.'

On the television, a message reading 'NO SIGNAL' was flashing. It came and went irregularly, with no obvious pattern. In the kitchen, the group was making appetizers; someone asked what needed doing, exactly, with the octopus. Aitana came and took over the remote-control duties, flicking through various sub-menus.

'Last year this weird thing happened to me while I was watching TV at my parents' house,' she said, while taking drags on her cigarette. 'They'd gone to bed, and I was on my own, lying on the sofa, watching rubbish. You weren't coming down that weekend, Carlos. I can't remember if I was watching *Equipo de investigación** or some film I'd seen a thousand times. It must have been around two in the morning. The ad break started, and I watched the first two adverts and then

---

* *Equipo de investigación* was a Spanish current affairs programme presented by Glòria Serra and shown on the late-night slot of the channels Antena 3 and La Sexta from 2011 until 2028, although it was later frequently repeated on the Nitro and Mega channels from the same media group.

changed the channel. On this new channel, an ad break also came on. The adverts started and they were the same adverts as on the other channel, in the same order. At that time of day, the ads are really trashy, right, and so it was all sports betting, aftershaves and home shopping: an air freshener, then a potato peeler, and then, in third place, some sort of contraption for exercising without moving a muscle. I changed channels twice more, and it was those same adverts again, in the same order. I thought, well, these channels are both part of Antena 3's multiplex, and all the channels must agree to go to adverts at the same time. But I flipped through five other channels and they were all showing exactly the same ads in the same order: gambling, aftershave, home shopping. I kept changing channels, and every single one had the same adverts. The strange thing, *really* strange, happened when I went back to the first channel, the one I was watching at the start, and the commercial break ended – it must have lasted, I don't know, around seven minutes. And then, instead of the programme starting again, the same block of ads began again. There was the same sports betting ad, again. I muted the TV and just waited in silence; all you could hear was the ticking of the clock in the kitchen. After the gambling ad it was the same aftershave ad again. I sat there, frozen. That's when I started to feel like something bad had happened, or was about to happen. I looked around, as if I needed to make sure there was no one else in the living room with me. I gave up trying to change channels and just sat there, stunned, confused – I couldn't stop staring at the screen, waiting to see if this endless loop of adverts would keep going. Then, there it was: after the aftershave, the air freshener appeared once more, the potato peeler and then the exercise device. I thought that if something bad really had happened, the TVs probably *would* broadcast a constant stream of the same block of adverts. Maybe in your screenplays, the end of the world isn't concealed behind a communication blackout but by exactly the opposite, and it's announced instead by a kind of cyclical, repetitive communication that's never suspended.'

Javier looked at Aitana as she continued to fiddle with the TV remote, stubbing her cigarette out in the ashtray. It was the first time I had heard this story.

'Then the transmission started up again and everything went back to normal; someone somewhere had made a mistake, they must have programmed something wrong and sent out the same block of ads twice. But it was disturbing, a really strange sensation, because everything was synchronized, all the TV channels were broadcasting exactly the same thing at the same time. Oh, there you go, we've got a signal now, you just had to retune the digital TV channels, the frequency's changed. The government put the radio spectrum out to tender again. You know, because the mobile phone operators are buying up the digital dividend.'

Aitana placed the remote control onto the stack of board games on the table and cracked open a bottle of beer. That year she had gone back to university and had begun working in a research group that was analysing the regulatory framework of the telecommunications market, so she knew what she was talking about. Although, to tell you the truth, she always knew what she was talking about.

'Let's cook this octopus, shall we?'

There they all were, sitting at the table. Enrique was working as an engineer at the offices of a Spanish company that made the components for air conditioners in Shanghai; Irena and Eduardo had met in Brussels, she a Polish lawyer for an NGO that focused on refugee rights, he a translator for a Franco-German cultural TV channel; Sandra and Jimena were sitting side by side, tickling each other: the former, a chemist in a laboratory that analysed food products, the latter a student doing a postgrad in immunodeficiency in pets (they shared a flat in Frankfurt and at that point were still a couple); Diana had left her job as a producer on a reality TV show a month ago – she had also left Madrid, and her relationship with Mario, and she was now at her parents' house recovering from temporary blindness caused by stress (the blindness had disappeared as quickly as it had arrived, but she was still under observation); Eric, downcast, had perhaps been working for too many years in the same Spanish tapas restaurant in Berlin, and it was rumoured that things were not going well with his Basque boyfriend; and Javier you already know, he was back in the capital after having spent two years unemployed in his parents' house in Murcia. The octopus had caused some problems. It was tasty and its texture was not tough or slimy, but neither Diana nor Javier, the two from Murcia who had been in charge of cooking it, wanted to try any of it. They said that *'the smell had got into their noses'.* My salads, meanwhile, enjoyed a reasonable amount of success. Pacheco had had a string of short-term posts: a job as a porter in a hotel in Lyon, some Spanish teaching in Manchester, then a fruitless attempt at volunteering for a charity in Nicaragua. He had studied journalism, like Aitana and me, and at the time was weighing up whether to go and live in a village while he retrained as a web content manager. Aitana was waiting to finish her doctorate after submitting her thesis on the evolution of local TV channels in Spain and their importance as a space for democratic plurality and community, channels that had been decimated precisely because of the licences for deployment of the ubiquitous DTT, which had replaced the snow of interference with a sleek, perfectly die-cut digital artefact. And lastly, there was me. I observe them, I listen, from a distance. I am there with them and I am also here, by your side. I am, once again, in two places at once.

'The skin was floating – is it normal for the skin to come off?'

'My dad used to install aerials, and he didn't have to retune the channels every single fucking year.'

'We might have overcooked it.'

'We can listen to the bells outside, on the car radio.'

'I think we're going to move out of Prenzlauer Berg.'

'No one wants prawns? Seriously?'

'We'll have the channels in five minutes: look, we're up to 680 megahertz now.'

'Asier's got a new job, we're thinking of moving to one of the neighbourhoods in the south.'

'Dystopia is always reactionary. You're shuttering the present against a terrifying future.'

'The local government used to cover my rent and the cat's food. Now that Asier's making contributions we'll have to get by some other way.'

'I don't know, to me utopia seems more reactionary.'

'A toast to the barbecue king!'

'To Pacheco!

'Hurrah for Pacheco!'

'Give us a dance, Pacheco!'

'To Carlos, Carlos, give the prawn heads to Carlos, he loves them.'

'Just full of pushchairs and organic shops. And people who do these upwards laughs. They don't know how to laugh, you know what I mean? They just look up and open their mouths.'

'What's a multiplex?'

'Fear always paralyses people. These films just spread fear around.'

'Well, I think the octopus is perfectly done.'

'Is there no scorpionfish cake left?'

'It's for breakfast, Carlos's going to make prawn toast for breakfast tomorrow.'

'I haven't read your screenplays, I'm just telling you what I've seen in those kinds of films.'

'The electromagnetic spectrum is finite. It occupies a limited range of frequencies, so there's a lot of competition over them.'

'Is it a cake or a paté? I'm never sure.'

'In *Take Shelter,** for example, in the final sequence we find out that the protagonist isn't mad: the catastrophe he was imagining proves to be real. That's what's reactionary, rewarding the paranoid person, the nutter who wants to lock his family up in a bunker.'

'When you digitize the signal you can include more channels. Before, you only had the UHF bands. You can fit around four channels in each multiplex now.'

'They don't pay for your electricity, not in Germany or here.'

'Ultra high frequency.'

'I suggest you take out the pips; look – split them open, like this. Otherwise, you'll choke.'

'The spectrum used to be State-owned, but it was deregulated in 2010. Now we're in a process of frequency redistribution. The band above 800 megahertz was sold to mobile phone operators.'

'I take the skin off, too. Eduardo – how do you say "piel de uva" in English?'

'Faster transmission speed and a more stable distribution; the lower frequencies go through the walls of buildings more easily.'

'*Skin*?'

'Who's Asier been hired by?'

'I don't know – for instance, watching a film on your phone when you're in the metro or on a train.'

---

* Thriller from 2011, directed by Jeff Nichols and starring Michael Shannon and Jessica Chastain.

'I'd rather go outside and eat the grapes with the car radio on, I'm serious.'

Twelve o'clock came around, we ate our grapes outside, hugged each other and opened the bottle of cava. We put on some music and made ourselves drinks. Irena and Eduardo decided to go for a walk around the residential development and we waved them off from the porch, the silence from the neighbouring properties enveloping us. Sandra snuck a prawn head into my gin and tonic and played a couple of other annoying practical jokes; I suppose this must be why she ended up pissing us all off so much and would, over the years, cease to form part of our lives, although Aitana has a different theory. Aitana was at that moment smoking with Diana in the garden, both women sitting out on the reclining chairs where just a few hours ago I had been trying to make out shapes in the darkness. Diana beckoned me over. Now that the new year had begun, and we had all raised our glasses and dined and celebrated, now that the last day had been handled without setback or disaster and we were all safe and gathered together, happy and serene, I tried hard to forget about the past and the future, determined not to worry or feel gloomy. We had arrived, we were together and that was the end of it. It was no small thing, given the turbulence all around us, and I would like to think that in those days up there in the mountains, surrounded by friendship, I found a stray, momentary sense of gratitude.

'We've got a situation and we don't know what to do.' Diana

was speaking with unexpected gravity while Aitana looked sidelong at me, sipping at the straw in her rum and Coke.

'I was going to wait until tomorrow to tell you, when everyone's a bit less drunk and emotional.' Aitana had a habit of protecting me from my tendency towards sentimentality, and I tried to reciprocate by protecting her, in turn, from her tendency to protect everyone else.

'Jimena ran into Asier in Berlin last week and he told her that he and Eric broke up four months ago. She was in town for something to do with the university, just for the day, which is why she hadn't told Eric she was there.'

'Has he said anything to you? Like, was he worried about how things were going?' Aitana stirred the ice in her drink.

Someone broke something inside the house; the dancing had started.

'No. I mean, he calls me all the time, but he mainly talks about his designs and his projects. He doesn't tell me anything personal – you know what he's like. He's done things like that in the past; he lies to us because he's constantly lying to himself.'

Eric was a combination of all the classic stereotypes of the Spanish émigré in Berlin with artistic aspirations and an urge for some sort of personal, professional or social 'break'. He had left just before the 2008 crisis, when everything still had a feeling of play and discovery about it. After a month or so, this 'break', as he called it, this reset in the face of the disappointments of youth, manifested not so much in a kind of turning point, regeneration or readjustment, as in a kind of deferral of the present. An existential moratorium, extra time with no final whistle, in which there was a suspension of responsibilities and obligations. Over the years, as it did for so many others like him, this broadened into a suspension of his age and its generational conditions, as well as of space, nationality and the way he belonged to a place – the suspension of time itself. His origins were suspended and, as a result and without him suspecting it, where he was headed was too, which placed the young migrant in an indefinite state of paralysis. The victims of this state, needless to say, numbered several thousand. This is also an affliction that looms over any long-term expatriate to some degree. But Berlin, at least in that distant, never-ending first decade of the twenty-first century, offered perhaps the most refined way to experience it. These émigrés found themselves, then, in a city with no escape route that provided them with amenities and living expenses and, above all, with a permanent, recyclable *sense of opportunity*: relationships, encounters, projects and art openings all saturated with a beguiling, rejuvenating euphoria (why an entire generation of twenty-something Europeans needed rejuvenating is a subject for another time). In any case, we should understand these openings not just as *vernissages* of experimental exhibitions, performances and short films, but rather as emblematic of their shared lifestyle: 'the *inaugural*' was the unmistakable promise of events that any adopted resident of Berlin experienced every morning upon waking up. This is not as capricious or as superficial as I have described it. Berlin provided an *atmosphere* that we might – depending on how we feel that day – classify as inspiring, welcoming, active, bohemian, seedy, self-absorbed or hypocritical. A domain, even if it was sometimes intangible, of proposals and possibilities, of trust and hope, a beaming attitude towards the future which was addictive because it was invaluable, given the paralysing depression and general listlessness that had settled over the societies and economies of southern Europe.

'Jimena went to see him in the bar where he works and they told her he'd quit before the summer.'

Diana was squinting a little, and I wondered if she'd done a line. Before I could remind them that Eric had done this kind of thing before and that he was probably just working in another bar where he didn't yet have any debts or bad vibes with anyone, and that he probably hadn't told us to avoid us lecturing him about it, Aitana said the magic words:

'But that's not what we're worried about.'

'Or it's not what we're *most* worried about. Jimena tried to talk to him when we got here. She was messing around and got into the shower with him when he was having a wash, and she saw that he had these marks.'

'Marks?'

'Scars. On his back. Some recent, some that were older.'

From the living room the sound of '90s merengue and bachata came floating out, abruptly punctuated by trap and reggaeton from our own decade. Aitana gathered up the fag ends, lured by the luscious melodies. As she walked past me, she pinched my bum.

'The thing is, Jimena's got a plan. But Diana and I aren't convinced it's such a good idea.'

*

We closed our eyes.

'Night falls, and in the village of Sotolix the townsfolk are all on their way to bed. It's been a long day and they're exhausted, but in the surrounding woods, evil forces are hiding. Shadows move through the cobbled streets. The hours go by, and the village sleeps peacefully. When the sun comes up, everything appears to be normal again; however, in a doorway, a dead body has appeared with its throat slit, lying in a pool of its own blood. The bloody body of . . . Diana!'

'Fuck you! You killed me first because you're scared of me, you bastards.'

Diana threw down her card; she was the Little Girl, which generated a collective mewling of dismay. The Little Girl was important. Enrique, with his deep bassy voice and his long brown beard, was acting as the Moderator, controlling timings, smoothing over confrontations, and directing the imaginary scene, as exciting as it was macabre, which we had opted to immerse ourselves in.

In The Werewolves of Miller's Hollow, each player receives a card that determines whether they are a villager or a werewolf; although the pack includes a few special characters, of these we had only included the Little Girl, who was the sole villager who could open her eyes at night and try to surprise the wicked wolves, and who in any case they had just killed off in the first round. Since there were eight people in the village (Irena and Eduardo weren't back from their walk yet), we gave out two werewolf cards. Each night – each round – the wolves would attack and kill one villager while the village slept. This meant that there were two wolves hidden among us. After the night's crime we had to discuss as a group who we thought the murderers were, knowing that the undercover wolves would try to throw us off the scent with false information. The reasoning in the discussion was unstable: someone would argue that they had heard something, another that they had picked up on a villager seeming quieter or more nervous than usual, while a third would be overcome by an intense, inexplicable intuition. Or we would all just yell and accuse each other, in the grip of a make-believe frenzy that could lead to a very real uproar. A very simple game, the most basic form of role-play which could, nonetheless, due to its group dynamic and its suspicious, fearful atmosphere of elimination, drift quite quickly towards a rather unfriendly tension, towards cruelty. It was very common during the deliberations for an innocent man or woman to be accidentally lynched by an enraged group of townsfolk, which was not always well received by the victim and would give rise to accusations of injustice or to revenge being sought for something external to the game itself.

'Someone's lying here.'

And this was the confused plan Jimena had concocted to unmask Eric: she would use the twisted dynamic of the game to make him confess in real time – a strategy that under no circumstances would be successful (its success could only mean a public takedown, an unpleasant, shameful humiliation). It seemed out of character for Jimena, who we didn't associate with either meddling or sadistic behaviour. So, Diana, Aitana and I guessed relatively easily that hiding behind an idea so incredibly adolescent, with results that were arbitrary and potentially destructive, could only be the worryingly sociopathic temperament of Sandra. Jimena – let's at least try to understand her – insisted that she had attempted to speak in private to the aforementioned man on several occasions and that he had repeatedly given her the slip. (Let's not forget that Jimena chased him into the bowels of a sofa.) Now, Eric had got all tangled up in another worrying web of lies (accusing Asier of having made it all up), which came dangerously close to a psychiatric diagnosis. And so the matter had become a goal for Jimena to accomplish, a monolith to tear down, which does not exactly speak well of her empathic qualities, either. On the night in question, the drunkenness and the New Year's enthusiasm prevented us from aborting the game. And while playing the game, Eric had no escape route.

'I think Eric's one of the wolves.'

'Well, I think it's you, Jimena.'

'Yeah, Eric looks like a liar.'

'You're a fierce little wolf, Eric.'

'You see how they're attacking me? Jimena and Sandra are the werewolves, it's obvious!'

'Come on, Eric, tell us the truth.'

'Wolves! Wolves! You look like wolves to me. Bitches and dykes, the both of you!' Eric was squirming nervously, pointing at the two girls with an easy mixture of aggression, lewdness and misogyny.

'Enough, Eric, no more lies.'

'Well, I think I heard Pacheco.' Aitana decided to intervene and relieve some of the pressure on her cornered friend.

The werewolves opened their eyes at night. As the rest of the village sat there blindly and quietly, the wolf players, their eyes wide open, had to decide who to kill and, with a wave of their hand, point out the victim to the games master, the stage manager. This sound, imperceptible, was often used by the true wolves to throw the other players off and peddle misleading clues. I intervened:

'How can you hear Pacheco if he's on the other side of the table? Maybe you're one of the wolves, Aitana?'

'I'm just saying that Pacheco here is very quiet.'

'He's keeping quiet so he doesn't lie.'

'There are liars all over the place.'

'It's Pacheco! It's Pacheco! He's gone all red!'

'To the bonfire with him!'

'I don't . . .'

'He can't even speak – murderer!'

'Quiet, please. How many votes for Pacheco? Raise your hands.'

'Wait, wait!'

'Well, I reckon it's Javier.'

'Never! Look at my hands, my teeth! I'm a human just like you!'

'Well, it reeks of werewolf in here – get a whiff of Eric, you guys.'

'Three votes for Pacheco.'

'Let me at least defend myself.'

'Who votes for Eric? Is it just us two? Carlos, Aitana, Javier: don't you think he's the wolf? Isn't there anything you'd like to tell us, Eric?'

'Yeah, Eric – don't you think it's time to show us your claws?'

The best – and also the worst – thing about this game is that there is no unequivocal strategy. Cunning does not ensure success, and nor does vehemence; no one tactic leads to safety. Every game is resolved using persuasion, and the deliberation (ending in an execution in the town square) is settled collectively, out loud and in broad daylight. Consequently, it is fun as well as unruly. The game turns us into a mass of incomprehensible fears, sympathies and alliances, and we might consider that they illustrate, if this game illustrates anything, the triumph of discourse over storytelling. At the end of every game, particularly if the wolves have gone undetected and end up gobbling down the last remaining local, a playful but ultimately uncomfortable atmosphere of lies and betrayal will end up hovering – prevailing, perhaps – among the group, with declarations such as the following being heard:

I don't want to die!
I refuse to die!
Why have you killed me?
We've bumped off an innocent person!
I told you!
You've tricked me.
You shouldn't have believed me.

No, it can't be you, please no, not you.
Now we're going to eat you.
I trusted you.
Prepare to die.
Help!

But this did not happen in this game. Instead, Enrique asked why Sandra and Jimena kept on at Eric, while Javier looked at me and Aitana in confusion, not understanding what was going on – the situation was frankly strange – and Aitana and I looked at each other, blinking like bewildered little animals, but helpless to resist Sandra and Jimena's plan. As Diana got up to pour herself another drink, determined to disassociate herself from all the emotion, Aitana and I prepared to raise our hands to execute Eric – adding two more votes to those of Jimena and Sandra – and I, forever anxious and ready for *the worst*, braced myself to hear Sandra say something like, 'Take off your shirt so we can see your scratches, you werewolf!' – something which she probably wouldn't have said ordinarily, but was driven to do so by the game, and which would no doubt nudge me into the depths of fright and physical discomfort. But just at this moment, Pacheco – who was sweating profusely and had turned a deep crimson – tossed his card down on to the table and broke the spell, stammering a little as he said:

'Fine, it's me, I'm one of the wolves. Kill me.'

Even I roared indignantly. This wasn't how you played the game, what was he thinking, we were still voting! Pacheco hadn't only messed up this round, he had ruined the whole game. He had delivered an open slap in the face in the full throes of proceedings, and if we had been a court that could condemn him to death, we would have ruled to do so in a millisecond, so deeply unacceptable do we find it when someone breaks a set of rules. So monstruous and uncivilized does it seem when someone breaks a fictitious agreement that has allowed us, for a few painless minutes, to act in an irreproachably monstrous way towards our friends. Pacheco had given himself away, had done that which should never be done, that which is never even *contemplated* ordinarily, and it wasn't a slip or because he didn't know how the game worked. He had decided to resolve the situation, to quash our rage and liberate Eric out of kindness, or – I can't rule it out – perhaps for more arcane reasons. And nor did we have time to look for an answer, because in the midst of this collective short-circuiting, Irena and Eduardo came in, flushed and happy, wearing coats, gloves and woolly hats, oblivious to our confusion, and with a spirited, adventurous suggestion:

'A lake, a lake – we've discovered a lake! You have to come and see it!'

So off we went. Irena and Eduardo took great pains to convince us we should all go. It wasn't far, they said, and it was unlike any lake any of us had ever seen before. And so, with this most unexpected, wonderful interjection, we ventured out into the cold of the wind and the trees. We walked through the darkness chatting animatedly, and didn't speak again of what had happened after dinner. A conflagration had been avoided, and the suspicions, at least for that evening, had melted away. We walked over wet leaves, following the beams of light from Irena and Eduardo's torches, and I think we were all grateful and content. Our guides were like excited children in possession of an incredible secret, hopping up and down and whispering. Diana, who had worked for several years in TV, was still interested in the ownership, sale and concession of the radio frequency, the finite nature of its space, the encrypted circulation of all those images and sounds flying around for which we lacked the decoding equipment. As we pushed deeper through ferns and pine woods, she and Aitana continued to talk about the legislation for the invisible and the monopoly of the visible; they talked about how the reflection and dispersal of energy created echoes and shadow zones in analogue transmission, which show up as snow, double images, burnt colours, buzzing or whistling, and how, at the same time, digital transmission can only correct interference up to a point, because the encryption isn't done proportionally.

'When the digital receiver isn't capable of rectifying certain errors, the image can freeze, or the sound might get cut off. If the level of error goes above a certain limit, the receiver is incapable of fixing the signal. That's when the screen shows a black image, with no sound. The fact that you have this fixed error limit and not a gradual decrease in quality is known as the "digital cliff effect", a phrase me and Carlos find really funny. Recently, we've been talking about "falling off the digital cliff" all the time.'

Diana was listening carefully, but she kept insisting that, despite having worked on news bulletins with mobile units, and even though she'd studied it, she still didn't understand it. What's more, she was convinced she never would.

'If you told me it was magic, if you said it's something that we were given by some supreme being and that human beings had nothing to do with it, that would seem just as plausible as an explanation, I'm telling you – I just can't wrap my head around it!'

After we had walked for half an hour, a glimmer through the trees stopped all of our conversations in their tracks; we emerged from the woods and, down in a hollow, we saw a dark and shimmering surface under the cloud-covered yellow sky, polluted by the lights from the motorway and surrounding villages. It was a lagoon rather than a lake, occupying a space the size of a football field, and causing the nocturnal light from overhead to swell, with flashes of crystal and diamond, as if the bottom of this lagoon held thousands upon thousands of precious stones. Irena and Eduardo ran down the bank and began to walk on the surface: the water appeared to be frozen.

'What do you think it is?' they called up to us from the mirage.

As we walked down the slope, the optical effect gradually dissolved, the jewels acquiring oily tones, floating on our retinas as blues, magentas and violets. Slowly, silently, we drew closer, unable to comprehend what we were seeing, despite the fact that we could by now see shards and edges, the objects and their lack of movement slowly coming into focus.

'Are they crystals?'

Irena and Eduardo laughed, fully immersed in the moment.

'We made the same face you're all making! Come on, come closer!'

Diana hung back, saying that it was giving her 'bad vibes'.

I walked over to Eric and Aitana, determined not to be left behind. Sandra was the first to reach the shoreline of this water that wasn't water, and we could hear the crunch of plastic beneath her boots. Irena instructed her not to reveal what was going on, to let us discover it for ourselves. Surprisingly, perhaps because she said it in English, or perhaps because she was firm with her (only someone as utterly charming as Irena could get away with being so firm), Sandra shut her mouth for once. Enrique squatted down and let out a soft chuckle.

'I thought so.'

I crouched down at the edge and picked up one of the reflective discs, turned it over and read, 'Paul Simon. *Graceland*'. I spotted another one with 'Adobe Acrobat 3.2' on it. Heaped up, strewn about, spread all across this dip in the landscape like a sheet of quartz, were thousands and thousands of compact discs,* glinting.

'Careful, we could easily cut ourselves.'

---

* The compact disc (or CD) was an optical disc used to store data in digital form, popularized halfway through the 1980s as a means of launching new musical releases and reissues, replacing the role the vinyl LP had played until then. In the early 2010s, CD sales declined with the appearance of other kinds of music players, file formats and internet platforms. Nowadays, their presence is largely peripheral and aimed at collectors.

We walked and ran across this mirror which was ice one minute, plastic the next, a thousand full moons one minute, a thousand new moons the next. We pretended we were ice skating. Aitana and I held hands and danced around, sketching out Ss and circles. We took hundreds of photos of us all swimming, and rowing in a make-believe boat, and holding hands in a long line. At some point, Eduardo and Irena crossed over with Pacheco to the other side of the artificial shore and started fiddling around with some rucksacks they had brought with them. They asked me to tell everyone else to go and sit on a large rock near the black conifer forest we had walked through to reach the CDs. Aitana was on her own, in the middle of the plastic and aluminium lagoon, and I ran over to her.

'They're asking us to go over to that bit of the lake.'

She looked at me and stood up without saying a word. As we walked over to where our friends were waiting for us, I felt as if I had interrupted her in some reflection that was a little less cheery than the situation we found ourselves in. When we sat down, waiting for the others to do whatever they had to do, she leant her head on my shoulder – something she very rarely did, because she is taller than me and my shoulders are pretty bony. We stayed like that for a moment or two and then she said:

'It's not a lake – it's a graveyard.'

Pacheco, Irena and Eduardo were running towards us. Then, fireworks started going off and we clapped and cheered at every rocket, Roman candle and Catherine wheel, for every fountain and streamer that crackled green, red and gold and then exploded into emeralds, rubies and sapphires over the still surface of the pond. This is how I remember us: as blissful as children, untroubled and ignorant of the dangers all around us, which in those years we weren't yet able to see, to name or to imagine.

V

THE HORIZON LINE

The landscape through the window was grey. A dark, grey desert. The night, always still, was always the same night; it had seemed to last too many days. The girls had just gone to bed, and I was washing up after dinner. Aitana stayed sitting at the table, puffing on her plastic cigarette. I understood, from her silence, that she was about to tell me something she had been keeping to herself all day. When I had finished drying and putting away all the plates and glasses, she cleared her throat and told me she had come across my brother last night, in a video game about military campaigns set in fifth-century Hispania.

'We were advancing at daybreak, through the mist; the attack on Begastri was planned for as soon as the first rays of sun appeared. I was commanding thirty *palatini*. We'd been walking for a while when, without understanding why, we found ourselves on top of a hill. The guides had become disoriented, and we'd accidentally ended up on a plateau with hardly any tree coverage. The mist was protecting us for the time being, but we were exposed. I was about to give the order to retreat when, through the mist, I saw a bright sign floating in the air and I recognized his name, Clodoveo81. I hadn't run into him since last year, since the defence of Tarraco. The sign loomed in and out of view through the wisps of fog. I moved forward alone, so that none of my own men would attack him. There he was, standing stock still, silent and alone, on this deserted summit in the middle of nowhere, a long way from his regiment of hunters. I thought he must have deserted, and then immediately thought that it didn't make much sense to desert in a strategy-based war game. I waved at him, and he didn't move, seeming not to see me. Then an arrow hit me: the Visigoths had been warned and were waiting for us. I was carried away and my people launched into hand-to-hand combat against the enemy units. In the middle of the battle, he was still there, motionless, oblivious to it all. It was the last thing I saw before they took me to the infirmary.'

'That's strange.'

'It is a little bit strange. Maybe he had a power cut and that's why he was kind of frozen or paused. But the soldier was definitely active. He was breathing.'

'He was breathing.'

'Or else I caught him on the toilet, I suppose. I wouldn't worry. Although you should probably write to him.'

We had heard nothing from my brother for several months. Ousted from the university in the extreme right-wing biennium, he had decided, at the age of fifty-four, to go and shut himself up in our family home. This had been a year or so ago. Our parents, sweet and calm, were in their retirement home on the coast and he, meanwhile, had decided to go and hole up in a holiday home deep in the province, situated on the edge of a residential development surrounded by desert and highways. The place we spent summers when we were children and where, according to his own personal mythology, he had enjoyed the happiest moments of his life. He had no children, was divorced, and had become distanced from his friendships in Valencia, so Aitana and I did not expect much from this plan aside from a carefully orchestrated dive into the oceans of depression, a depression that I foresaw as contagious. The long emails he sent me, in which he presented himself as a Robinson Crusoe of his own mind, explorer of our family's memories and archaeologist of our childhood and adolescent universe, could easily end up destroying me, too. Destroying my patience, my happiness, or both. Comments such as, 'I've managed to connect the Mega Drive to the flat screen' brought out the nervous anxiety that my brother's arbitrarily melancholy – or, in this case, voluntarily melancholy – temperament always induced in me whenever he went into 'retro' mode. Our lives were not made – no lives were, truth be told – to settle into regulated, manageable bouts of deliberate sadness. Perhaps reading his words bothered me because they were a reminder of who I am, or of who I have chosen not to be. And so I read these diary entries (they could be thought of as a diary) rapidly and without paying too much attention, replying briefly and promising myself that one day I would read all of it slowly and reply with love and compassion, especially since, in the last few emails, he had started to describe, in a somewhat vague and confused manner, a type of eye condition or neurological illness that I couldn't understand and that I hadn't taken all that seriously, either. And so, after Aitana and I hugged each other goodnight, I sat down at the computer and, before replying, I began to read for the first and last time everything he had written to me.

20th July

My dear brother! How's everything going over there? I hope you're all still OK. The little news we get about your project is always cause for celebration. I always had faith in the two of you. Always. Don't stop sending me photos, please – send me as many as you like.

And in exchange, I promise not to send you any. After all, I imagine you're not that keen on me showing you this place again, and probably neither of you want to see how I'm starting to acquire a wan, haggard sort of look to my face, or how my loose and puffy flesh speaks to my decrepitude (my *idleness,* as Grandma would say). (I'm trying to write like you. Can you tell? We'll see how that goes!) Joking *aside* (not sure if I'm using italics properly there?), I won't send you photos. I don't want you to be able to see the inevitable deterioration I imagine you were expecting to happen to me. Instead, I will write to you. I'll write to tell you whatever I see and whatever happens to me here, in our old house. I'm not going to try and disguise what I'm doing, which we might rashly characterize as selfish, to make it look like a gift or an offering. I had thought about trying to convince you that, in telling you of my new life here, I could remind you of our shared memories, that I could recover our shared landscapes for you, our adventures together. (How much 'new life' is there in that, I hear you ask.) I wondered if I might convince you that I was writing to you for your own good – that I was preserving, and thus protecting, our past. But I understand perfectly that, as far away as you are and without any prospect of returning, you won't particularly appreciate me taking pleasure in – delighting in, even – emotional landscapes you can no longer visit and which, let's be clear, never really interested you – never really meant anything to you. You were always able to look unceremoniously towards the future. Perhaps you had no other choice. You've never (and your stories are proof of this) confused the future with the past, at any rate. And perhaps I am guilty of doing just that, but don't go thinking that I've come back here just to escape into comics, video games and other nostalgic enterprises – I have projects!

The truth is, I have to write to you because you're the only one I can talk to about the things that surround me. You're the only one I can share these days with. So, this correspondence is, to a large extent, a favour I am asking of you.

Earlier today, I parked the car down at the bottom of our bit of land and opened the gate. I went over to the orchard and saw that the lemon trees and the fig were hanging on; another two fruit trees (I don't know what they are) had completely dried up, though. There wasn't a trace of the mint or the parsley, both scorched by the sun. The truth is, I expected to find everything in a much worse state. They cut off the water for irrigation over a month ago, around the time I took Mum and Dad to the old people's home. I walked up the almost sheer slope, trying not to slip on the needles that drop from the big pine tree up top, forming a thick, dry carpet that I will sweep and clear away properly at some point. Little palm trees, ones our other grandmother would describe as *bordes*, feral, were dotted around the embankment that leads up to the house. I need to cut them and pull them up before the rats take them over, although I do like them. There is still bougainvillea, purple and pink, hanging down around the front door, and those other flowers, the red and yellow ones, that look like the Spanish flag – what are they called? What did Mum use to call them? Lantanas? Crespinillo? Pittosporum?

I got to the first set of steps, and before climbing them, I glanced over at the garage, which looks more like a storehouse, filled with the shelves and boxes where all our textbooks and school reports are kept, a folded-up ping-pong table, our rusty bicycles, board games and a lawn mower that must have gone thirty years without mowing any lawns. Lilos and plastic balls for the swimming pool were piled up in a corner, underneath the water heater. They were still inflated, surprisingly. I wondered who had inflated them and how many years they'd had this air inside them.

But I don't want to give too many *moribund* (I'm doing this italics thing wrong, aren't I?) descriptions – let's carry on up the steps. I reached the entrance to the house, surrounded by a perfect, radiant stretch of artificial grass, which gleamed so brightly it hurt to look at it. It was by far the most lush, fresh-looking thing in the whole plot of land, the most unquestionably vegetal. But when I stepped on it, it made a crunchy sound. It was boiling hot. My shoe stuck to it and I thought the sole had melted, but it was the blades of artificial grass that had melted; they were stuck to the bottom of my shoe. I hope to sort this out soon. That is, get rid of it. As I said before, I have plans. I was now standing before the pool, also green, but a different tone. I took shelter from the sun under the pergola over the front door and filled my lungs, trying to pick out some of the floral scents all around the house, but all I breathed in was dust and a smell I have always associated with the sun and which I guess must be the smell of the brick, the stones and the earth, scorched by this burning heat which, I have to say, I have really missed. Those yellow, dusty smells gave me the welcome that I had wanted.

Before going into the house, I walked all the way

around it, delaying my entrance, submitting to the sheer, overwhelming heat. In my opinion, it is the thing that best encapsulates this homeland of ours. A few small blue bell-shaped flowers were hanging from the vines that are slowly devouring the pine tree, which is the only source of shade left on that side of the house. Further on, some little pink and white flowers were fluttering sluggishly. If my memory serves me right, they belong to the Lady of the Night – or is it Queen of the Night? Or Don Pedro? Or Don Diego, perhaps? I can hardly remember any plant names. And I don't know if learning them now will be of any use to me. At the end of the day, who actually knows the varieties now? What does it matter if I leave them unnamed, when there are no flowers where you are? Read one of the novels from the nineteenth century and they're just a succession of flora and fauna, and those are precisely the passages that say nothing to us now. Does it matter if I'm surrounded by lavenders or honeysuckles without knowing what they are? Is naming things the only way of preserving them? Does a richer lexicon bring about a more varied world? I suspect that each age, each generation develops its own riches. And for us, naming flowers involves an unnecessary amount of effort.

I opened the door to the ground floor and the first question I asked myself caught me by surprise: where did I want to sleep? In my room? In our parents' bedroom? My feet gave me the answer, setting off, without any direction from me, for your bedroom. I put down my suitcases there and since then, I have been sitting at your desk writing this email, which is just about coming to an end.

Hugs from your loving brother.

24th July

Carlos, Charly, my younger-older brother, this is your older-younger brother writing. I'm writing again, without giving you time to reply, since, as you can probably tell, things *keep happening to me*. This morning, I had my last dip in the pool. Shortly afterwards, I showered and scrubbed myself. (The truth is I only dared put my legs in: I didn't trust the algae and bacteria not to give me some kind of infection.) It was a swampy 'bathing' experience. And it was the perfect way to say goodbye to our swimming pool after four decades of service. After my morning dip, I went over to say hello to Fátima, and to ask her how she and her daughter had managed to drain their own pool. When I told her that I had permanently moved here, she looked at me with her big round eyes, welcomed me and said that she was glad to have a new neighbour, although her face did not contain any emotion, positive or negative, that I could make out.

From what I've read, even though it's chlorinated I can still use this water on the plants, as long as it doesn't exceed certain chemical indicators or contain algaecides (which, judging by the fact that it's the colour of cream of spinach soup, it doesn't). I've also been told that there are some new local government subsidies you can get for each new tree planted; I need to look into that, too.

The fact is I've been quite busy setting up the irrigation system, and with cleaning, purchasing provisions, getting the bedroom ready (I'm sticking with yours, as it's the coolest). I still haven't decided whether to throw anything out or to leave everything as it is. The truth is that the house has hardly changed a bit in all these years. The evening I arrived it startled me to have my memory laid out before me. The shelves in the living room and the study upstairs are still filled with endless volumes of 'adult' sci-fi comics (*Totem, Cimoc, Zona 84*) and all of the sci-fi and fantasy novels that Dad bought over many years (collections of books published by Nova, Ultramar, Orbis, Gran Super Ficción) and which I read during all those summers I used to spend here, without any friends, and without the desire to make any, accompanied only by a little blond kid five years younger than me, with whom I found a magic talisman in an emerald grotto, with whom I defended a fortress besieged by bat-monkeys, with whom I invented new sports: aquatic hide-and-seek, trampoline basketball, suit-of-armour handball. How many metamorphoses has this house gone through? How many different dens, citadels, aircrafts has it become? If we were to make an imaginary map of the land outside and all the surrounding areas, how many islands, how many continents, how many worlds would it contain? The truth is that the house always looked a little like a castle, despite its style – a rural villa, typical of the early '90s. Its three-tiered façade, formed of three maroon-coloured blocks, meant it was visible from the motorway, several kilometres off, from the town, and even from the train that took me to Valencia every year. I've always thought it fortunate that this house, perched as it is on the hill that marks the edge of the housing development, can be seen from so many places, and that from it, we can see almost half the province.

Did you know that, after he retired, Dad started re-reading all those novels and comics? He said he couldn't remember any of them; that it was as if he was reading them for the first time. I have to admit that one of my plans here was – is – to retrace my steps and play the video games from that period again, rewatch the series and films and re-read those books. I know you'll think I'm wallowing in some idealized past, but I'm not. Rather, it's an attempt to find another frequency, to reappraise those maps, and find new doors to go through.

As a teenager, I read those books, all of which Dad recommended to me. And now, I plan to re-read them, just as he did. Is to imitate our father to inhabit his life? Is it a means of ensuring that we reside in the same universe of fiction? Am I some kind of clone of him? An outgrowth, a fascicle? You were always closer to Mum and all her activities. I remember that you used to work in the kitchen and the garden with her while Dad and I would nod off reading magazines, or we'd sit and play the guitar or 'run errands' and slip off to the bar for a few beers on the way. This tendency towards idleness and, equally, towards melancholy is, as you have always reminded me, a privilege. Melancholy requires time; it requires, shall we say, *work*. You yourself refused to write for many years, because to you, the privileges – of gender, of class – bound up in this house, those summers, those tranquil stretches were hard to bear. They did not seem like something to which you *had a right*, but merely something that emanated from our condition as middle-class male children. The fact that you were able to transmit this idea to Dad and to me without sounding condescending is something that still amazes me. In another way (with far more warmth!), Aitana too woke us up to our privileges (she is probably the person who has taught this family the most). I suppose you decided to write those stories once a good many of your privileges had disappeared or been taken away from you. We'll talk about Mum some other day. I suppose I want to reassure you that 'melancholy' isn't on my agenda here. Rather, I'm hoping to recuperate our imaginary worlds. Must the imagination really be melancholy after a certain age? I don't think so – the imagination isn't some childish instinct.

Talking like this, I imagine you'll be wondering if I have received any *visitors*. No, not yet, I haven't got *that deep* into the house. While it's true that I've had a few walks around upstairs and have taken a look at the curved balconies on one side of the first floor, I haven't noticed a presence nearby or heard any voices. That's why I'm re-reading everything and re-playing all these fantasy RPG games (I managed to connect the Mega Drive to the flat-screen TV!), to get on the right wavelength, to see the house again in its full dimension, or rather, in all its many dimensions.

So here I am, focused on my little rituals, while trying not to be a slave to them. I open and close windows, raise and lower blinds with punctual regularity, depending on where the sun is, so as to keep the house nice and cool. I eat my breakfast and dinner in the living room, protected from the incendiary heat, just as we've always done. Did I ever tell you that, during those summers, when I used to stay inside the house all day, I would play at making the afternoon last forever? Perhaps we did it together? Though, I don't think so – it feels like something I did alone. In fact, I remember this now that I'm writing to you. I remember that I would play this game when you all went to see Grandma at the beach while I, for whatever reason, stayed behind on my own in the house. You'll remember that our house has its back to the rest of the development, has its back to the twilight, while the front is open to the steep sides of the ravine and the desert. After religiously watching the sunset, I would go back inside the house, down to the living room on the first floor or to one of the ground-floor bedrooms. The light would fade, but slowly, and I would try to extend the violet gloom for as long as possible, without switching any lights on. Switching a light on meant the beginning of the night, and the end of the day. The artificial light created a boundary, thereby forcing me to confront the darkness outside. The nights can be complicated and sinister in this house, which is so isolated, so exposed, suspended over the valley and the pitch black of the desert. Starting the night meant plugging in the TV or the radio, cooking, turning on all the electrical appliances, filling everything with noise so the darkness wasn't overwhelming. Similarly, I have always been grateful for the highways that cross the horizon on the other side of the valley. Although the sea is far from here, the headlights and distant engines provide a constant murmur that one might associate with waves. And so, I would hole up while the house grew dark – though not *entirely dark* – and delay the evening. Dusk, that strange hour, saddened me and filled me with death. Even then, though I was scarcely aged twenty, it foreshadowed so many future solitudes. And so there I would be, happy and horribly paralysed, with no light to read, no video game to play, no television to turn on, in silence, looking out at the sky or the trees, wandering around the house bumping into chairs, which I could no longer make out in the darkness. And I suppose I was waiting for something, waiting for something to happen or for something to be revealed to me, something that exists only here, in this house, in that light.

Now, as soon as evening comes, I go for a walk along the paths in the ravine or through the housing development. It was probably the memory of these activities (that are decidedly moribund) that has led me to withdraw from the house when the light wanes. Although, to tell you the truth, I still haven't solved the problem of what to do with the house during these hours. Dusk still seems like the most dangerous point in the day to me. I'll tell you why. The first evening I got here and went out for a walk, something happened to me – something unexpected, something that's quite silly, but has also come to define my stay here. (How long I will remain here is a question I'm not going to ask myself.)

I left the development, exiting through the second, outer wire fence, and walked down through the slippery, rocky slopes that lead to the ravine and its 'green path', where the signs indicating the flora and fauna are (celebrating, you know, the famous biodiversity of the desert), and which are now black and cracked, burnt to a crisp by the sun. I didn't come across anyone on that stony slope (the ground covered with scree – zahorra, which is how this terrain has always been described – that word I do remember), and I discovered that on the mountainside opposite lots of pine trees had come down, uprooted by last autumn's floods. This gave the dark black woods on the hills opposite the house, when seen from a distance, the look of a cemetery or perhaps a battlefield, with all these bewildered, fallen trees, looking like they still had no idea what had happened to them. And I glimpsed other remains, too: an abandoned car, broken bricks and buckets of cement, cartons of wine and a dusty sofa, covered, I imagined, in spiders' webs. The landscape had also changed on my side of the ravine. I had to jump over a twisted, broken tree trunk and circumvent a part of the path that had been crushed, broken into pieces, buckling under the force of the deluge. New craters in a landscape where, year after year, mountains have been toppled or plains opened up. I walked down into the gorge. The feeling of a lunar, or Martian, landscape grew more pronounced as I observed the vultures' nests up high, black lairs on the walls of yellow rock. The riverbed, too, looked pale and cracked down below. I left the ravine before I reached the quarries and the cliffs, turning back into the development, this time via the northerly edge, the most scarcely populated area, the one that had been left half-finished. I walked up some steps covered with weeds and came out on a road that hadn't even been given a name. A succession of streetlights leading nowhere. The long slope, a tarmacked track with pavements but no houses, came to an end at the highest point of the development. I walked uphill sweating, exhausted by the heat, but going at a brisk pace because I wanted to see the sunset. It was an evening of African winds and haze rising from the agricultural land in the distance. Dad would say that the air was *fosca*, Mum that it was *calima*, though I don't know if those words say anything about this space and this light.

When I reached the end, the tarmac disappeared into

an expanse of rocks and scrub. The development abruptly halted at this point from which you can make out the entire region. I had missed the sunset. In the distance, the blue mountains shimmered beneath the airborne dust. To the right, everything was golden, and further to the right everything was orange. I could see four mountain ranges, one at each point of the compass: La Pila, Ricote, Espuña and Carrascoy. Down below, the nearby towns glinted – El Hondón, Los Puntales and Molinos del Río – scored with roads and smaller streets, dotted with industrial estates flecked with solitary lampposts and more housing developments like ours, all surrounded by whitish areas: wastelands, orchards and rubbish dumps. A landscape I knew by heart, but which on that evening was more obscured, submerged in that enduring mist that blurred the edges of everything and made the mountains disappear within a kind of dirty humidity which seemed to fog up my own eyes, too. Droplets of sweat fell from my eyelids.

At the same time as I contemplated this landscape, I was aware that something was observing me in turn. I felt a presence at my back, one which hadn't taken its eyes off me as I ascended the hillside. At no point did it cross my mind to turn around, for I knew – I have always known – that the gaze I felt behind me came from the other end of the development, from the southerly hill. It was the gaze of our house. I had climbed all the way up the path without daring to turn around – without daring to come face to face with the house at a distance, knowing it would be looking at me. You're going to think that I'm letting myself get swept up in strange obsessions, but let me explain. Those summers when I shut myself up for days at a time in our house, I didn't always stay shut up inside playing at making the evening last forever; sometimes the claustrophobia would start to suffocate me and I would go out on my bike into the dusk until I reached that same point. And I would wait until it grew dark, calmly staring at that same landscape, which was no more than a blurry cobweb today, and then, when I set off for home again, I would see it, I would see it there on the hillside facing me, somehow both near and far away, and I was perfectly capable of imagining its interior, empty and in semi-darkness, waiting for me. The house was waiting for me. And then a cold sweat would run down my back. The sensation that cowed me at that moment was utterly callous: when I saw the house in the distance as the evening drew to a close, knowing there was no one there, all I could think was that you were all dead. That the house was a coffin. This was, of course, no more than a teenage hallucination, but I'm sure you'll understand why I reserved a certain amount of precaution when it came to raising my head and looking in that direction today. What if I saw the house and all those solitary fears were reactivated? There would be nothing for it but to pack my suitcases and get the hell out of there.

I turned around, slowly. I decided to look. I'm not a teenager any more, after all. To my surprise, the house wasn't there. For a moment I fancied that there was no ground beneath my feet. The house, which I knew exactly how to locate on the southerly hill, a couple of kilometres away, was not where it ought to have been. It wasn't anywhere. In those few seconds of bewilderment, I felt a little like I was outside time and space, as if displaced, as if expelled from where I was and lost in an unknown location. Then, once I had got over this intense initial bafflement, I realized that the few trees that have remained standing, ours as well as those of the neighbours, have grown over the years until they have entirely blocked our house from view. It is now hidden; it can't be seen any more.

As I was walking back, I explored other angles and perspectives, trying to find some trace of its presence, which, when I resist these adolescent terrors, is always warm and poignant, a reminder of happy moments. As it was night-time by that point, I decided to go back through the centre of the housing development. Along the way I heard families, chatty and industrious, getting ready for dinner. People still live here, and this sound of pans, of food being fried and cutlery clinking, calmed me down and reminded me that, whatever happened, I was back in my home. From time to time, as I turned the corner of one of the streets, I thought that I saw our house peering out between the other houses and I admit that I raised my hand, like a child, to wave at it. 'Hello, house.' And so, I returned home, my mood matching the warm, amniotic temperature of summer nights, until I let myself be swept up in a new worry: if the house can no longer be seen from anywhere, what can be seen from the house? Only trees and sky? Have I lost the lovely views of the surrounding landscape? Gradually I sped up, toying with the idea of pruning, or cutting down, even, some of those hulking trees which were now stopping me from seeing and from being seen. I would explore whether this might form one of my future projects. As I told you before – I have plans.

Big hug to everyone. I promise I won't write so much in future communications!

P.S. When I got home that night there were other surprises waiting for me. Fátima and her daughter (I can never remember her name) were having guests over. They had organized a meal, and later that night they started singing and playing the guitar. I listened to them from the terrace while I ate my dinner; a breeze got up at last and cooled the day down. I sat in silence, peacefully, listening to songs I didn't know and enjoying the magnificent nights we get here. Suddenly, from below, up floated the smell of the flowers. They only give off their sweet, fresh scent at night. We're not completely ruined, Carlos.

30th July

Haze, haze, and more haze – how long is this going to last? We haven't seen the sun for almost a week. The days go from grey to grey. The sky looks like the dirty water from a washbasin. The villages and far-off highways are shrouded in mist, a dust that looks like smoke that looks like dust. The far-off peaks and hills are just a faint veil. The landscape is forever on the point of disappearing, although it never does so entirely. You can't make out the horizon, so the land and the sky look pasted on, or saturated maybe, I don't know. I hope to improve my metaphors and not use the word 'washbasin' in future correspondence.

A short email about how you're all getting on would be welcome. But I don't want to bother you either; who knows – maybe you're on holiday? (Do you get holidays there? Does the month of August mean anything in that place?)

6th August

Just a quick note to say thank you for your last message. I'm glad to see the family are all happy. Tell me about you, though. Are you doing OK?

I'll be brief today. Last night I remembered something I wanted to tell you. Although, well, now that I'm here, I'll tell you how these past few weeks have been. Don't run away, please! Keep on reading! At the end of this letter a miracle is performed.

I wrote that I've been here 'for weeks'. I need to check on the calendar how much time has gone by. On the one hand it feels like I got here two days ago, but on the other,

I have the feeling that I've been here for months. I've got used to this house so fast. It's not that I'm getting bored or anything like that. It's just that it feels like I've been here a long time. In a way I've been here my whole life, haven't I? This house has always been inside me; I would wait all year long for the summer to arrive to return here, as if the rest of my life were an interval, a dream or, I don't know, a purgatory I had to cross in order to be able to get here every year. I wonder what I imagined was waiting for me and why I was so keen to come.

You know what, forget what I said about purgatory, I don't know why I wrote that, it gives the impression that I haven't lived, that I have only half lived, and that simply isn't true.

The swimming pool is empty now, the irrigation pipes repaired, the little palms dug up, the rats poisoned. Some nights I go up to the edge of the pool and I remember how as a teenager I would sit here at one or two in the morning, with you all asleep inside and all the lights switched off. The pool looked like some mountain lake and its surface, all black, reflected the stars. Over the years they built new branches of motorways, plus the capital and the surrounding cities expanded, and the stars vanished and the very blackness of the sky disappeared, tainted by the light pollution. I have remembered this these last few weeks, as the cloud cover has created a bell jar of humidity and dust which now surrounds us here. The sky, by day just as by night, has been white, whitish, off-white, chalky; it changes from a watery white to a pale grey. In any case, regardless of this recent cloud cover, the sky has seemed overcast at night for decades now. The houses and habits of the million people who populate the Gran Vega lend it a dull kind of clarity, between yellow and grey in hue. Fortunately, we can't see the mass of dwellings; we are protected by dark hills and the breaks in the ravine. But we do see the light they give off, or the sum of their light. And so, the swimming pool, at night, has for years reflected only a pale mass: its surface went from a starry blackness to the colourless light of the sky, the colour of things with no colour. Until now. Now that the pool has no water it is once again a black pit. A pool of night without stars.

I tentatively stepped down into the bottom of the pool, where nothing could be made out, and the darkness seemed neither oppressive nor abysmal. Next week I'll fill it in with earth: I've decided to turn it into a vegetable garden. That's one of my projects, which I've ended up telling you about too soon, although I suppose you were imagining it; it's what most of the families still here have done. Before long I will be able to float in a swimming pool filled with earth. But for now, I'll settle for sitting on the edge at night, my legs dangling, occasionally glancing at the house in the dark, its three storeys rising up before me.

I thought yesterday about how easy it is to see ghosts, to imagine that through the window of an unlit room a silent, pale spectral figure will emerge. Although, if you think about it, ghosts never 'emerge', ghosts are simply there already, waiting for you to see them. Ghosts are always on the lookout, ready to come across your gaze. The ghost is always still, observing, waiting. It is a presence that is already settled into the home, it does not need to invade it. It is a presence that, as a general rule, was residing there before we ourselves arrived. An inner assailant. In ghost stories, people almost always discover that the ghosts are the previous owners who want to trap them inside the house or oust them from it. Terrifying, no? That there might be some prior thing in the place that ought to be your home, your lair, your refuge. I did wonder, as I dangled my legs in this lake of nothingness, if there might not be some sort of middle-class neurosis encrypted in this collective fear. Are there ghost stories in societies where private property doesn't exist? Would there be ghosts in a commune, in a kolkhoz, in the cell where you guys live? The fear is quite recognizable (the past-tense inhabitant, hidden among your things, dead and at the same time alive), but we don't speak of how it's focused on property and ownership. What is someone doing in my house? Who is inside this sacred space? Is it possible that my house doesn't belong to me? That some pre-existing forces, legitimate proprietors of this space, my space, could demand it back? All this has only now occurred to me, now that I've made my peace with the house. The nights are calm here. Surprisingly calm. It might be because this house was built by our parents. I feel like I'd need to try really hard to see a ghost. Or, the ghost would have to really make its presence felt for me to wake up.

I was expecting a bit of anxiety and tension at night, at least at first, until I got used to the sounds of this huge three-storey house, so isolated, so outside the nucleus of families from the inner part of the housing development. We're still only three houses on this street. But the truth is that I sleep like a log. I listen to the distant car engines on the motorway, scattered dog barks and the odd nocturnal bird, and I just crash out. I was perhaps a little scared that burglars would get in at first, but that's eased since I found your baseball bat. The other visitors, the ones I am waiting for, have not yet graced us with their presence. I'm not afraid of them either. They are old friends and tend to come in the day.

I've left the fright I got last week till the end. An early-morning fright. A miraculous fright. Like I said, I'm still thinking of giving the trees on our land a good prune. The people who are bringing me a truckload of earth for the pool are going to help me with that. You may think this seems like an impulsive decision, but it also arises from necessity – the trees can't grow to a monstrous size, they might develop diseases, block out each other's light, their branches and leaves might bother the neighbours, although it's true that Fátima hasn't complained, and the people who live on the other side still haven't showed up. Perhaps it's a good idea, hygienic, for new light to enter the corners of this house. And yes, it's true, I admit that I want to be able to see once more the distant mountains, the valleys and the industrial estates from the windows and the terraces, I want to feel like someone is here with me.

So, I started to inspect the condition of the trees on the highest part of our land, the northern edge. I came across a veritable palisade of dark and dusty cypress trees, covered in cobwebs. Tightly packed and intertwined with one another, they looked like old men with sad eyes and beards so dense that their trunks were indistinguishable from one another. The trees themselves seemed inseparable, standing straight like a single wall of ancient branches. Out of curiosity, I pushed my hand very gently in among the little fleshy shoots of the leaves, and after an arduous tussle with the cobwebs and dry branches, found the trunk. I only had to place my hand on it to tell that it was hollow, dead. I pushed, ever so slightly, and the tree fell away from me, without making a sound, without a sigh. I stood very still, holding my breath. When the dust had settled, I stepped over to the other side. A three-metre tree, collapsed onto the neighbour's tennis court. It could have crushed someone; luckily, however, the house is still seemingly abandoned and there wasn't any major damage. Without thinking (I swear I didn't think about it), I grabbed two more trunks with both hands and pushed. The first tree fell easily, and the second one sort of *drooped*, clinging to its neighbour, without falling over completely. I went down to get some tools and a wheelbarrow, and when I got back, the entire palisade had come down. It had collapsed on to our plot. It could have crushed me, but it waited respectfully until I had left.

Behold the miracle: the miracle of my survival, or the miracle of my destructive power. The house is now partly liberated, its northern limit perfectly visible from the edge of the development. This event didn't worry me; I didn't feel in danger. On the contrary: I couldn't stop laughing. I cut up the branches and the trunks and carried them down to the skip, whistling and singing happily. I even began to think that I could change tack and use the water we had set aside for irrigation to fill the swimming pool up again. That way everything really would be like it was before! The trees would fall down one after another from lack of water and I would be able to swim and float on the surface just like before. If I wasn't sure that someone would report me, I'd try it. Although, who's going to report me given no one lives over on this side? Are they still doing drone inspections? What do you reckon, Carlos? Shall I risk it? I might end up behind bars! Again! Though, at least this time they'd be arresting me for a good reason . . .

2nd September

Summer is nearly over and no one has come. I haven't had a single visit. Not one door has opened. Mr Sartorius hasn't left me a single message, and nor have the Huntress Sisters, nor the Society of Wizards. You know who I'm talking about, right? You remember them? I'm sure, or almost sure, that you were there with me, with us, finding treasure, concocting spells, trying to read maps in the tavern. The tavern! I've looked for the map of that great inn, but I can't find it, and I can't remember now which of the rooms in this house was the tavern. I did find the folders. The little bits of card with our drawings on, the amulets on strings, the bag of marbles and the illustrations of all our swords and shields. The suits of armour aren't here – they must have been destroyed in the sixth war, the one against the underworld. When you do eventually write back to me, tell me, please, if you remember this; I'm convinced we shared all these imaginings, but the directions on the maps are only in my handwriting.

But yes, you were there, you were there! I remember you by my side at the battle of Mazmoria. I remember quite clearly that together we killed that gigantic troll in the swimming pool, which was a pond, which was a lagoon with a beautiful waterfall. We were together, and not just in this house and its multiple transmutations, but outside, too. Finding passageways, burying relics, setting traps, patrolling the movements from the Razed Tower and defending the Route of the Carolingians: the realm of adventures extended to the rest of the development, the ravine, the hills and woods that bordered us.

But since being here, since re-reading the comics and the sagas of dragons, since replaying *Wonder Boy V* and *Landstalker*, and listening to the records and watching the films from back then, I've also started to doubt my memories. I've begun to doubt whether we really did leave the house to walk along all those paths and sneak into other people's houses. I remember every corner being a riddle, every house an enchanted castle or an enemy fortress. But now I can't be certain. Did we really go out to have adventures? Did we really risk running into a neighbour who might take us for mad or weird children, talking to ourselves and crouching down behind hedges? Perhaps we never actually moved, never actually left the house? Did we run along roads and over bridges, did we hide in caves and discover hidden passages between the houses, or did I just imagine all this from the vantage point of the house, our watchtower? Perhaps I have to climb up to one of those vultures' nests to find the bag containing all of our most important maps. The one that contains all the most brightly coloured, precious marbles, the one we hid for the future, thinking we'd never forget the things in it: the maps of the tavern, the great inn, the Company's hideout and the tree fortress. I dream of finding that bag, buried under a black rock, so that it might lead me to the experiences I am struggling to conjure up, to the exact cartography of our memories.

Reply when you can – do you remember? Were you there? Did I tell you about it, at least? Sometimes I don't know what I've told you and what I have experienced with you. What I've expressed and what has remained inside me.

For many years, as soon as I arrived here, I would see not just the house, but all the versions of this house it had been. I was steamrollered by an accumulation of images. Of course, I remembered moments we had had as a family, with all of you, I remembered those, but the images I saw around me were mostly the memories of imaginary experiences. And it wasn't exactly an internal, mental activity, because more of these memories came alive with each step I took. And so I don't know whether to even call them 'memories'; they were more like snapshots of the past continually developing all around me. Nor did they appear in succession, but rather all at once, continuously, with no separation, a multitude of disorganized temporal layers all in one sudden jolt. So, there was no separation in my memory – in my perception – between what had happened and what had been imagined, because the imagined *had* happened, it had been experienced. My perception was my memory, and my memory was my perception. Each element of this house, each corner, each object, each *hour of the day,* each modulation of the light, each colour of the sky and each variation in the density of the temperature and the atmosphere was associated with an expansive proliferation of adventures, stories and characters, ceaseless and tumultuous.

I saw, heard and smelt all of this; it was staggering but not wearing, given that I enjoyed the intoxication and the vertigo of being surrounded by this multiplicity. No space was simply a space. Rather, it was a web of connections . . . No, not a web. Imagine a screen on to which are being projected, on top of each other and at the same time, millions of films. These films have no beginning and no end, and the screen surrounds you completely. Each area of the screen was at once hundreds of different spaces. That is what was waiting for me there and that is what I thought I could recreate by returning to this house. To be reunited with my internal and external projections, fuelled by all the fictions I have lived in this house. I hadn't fully realized until now, but this house is, or was, a kind of temple to fiction. Because, over the past few weeks, I have established that I can no longer conjure up these experiences. I spend my days trying to reanimate the memories, when all I can do now is visit them, like a tourist from the past. The memories are still there, but the fantasies no longer come to life. For instance, I can remember very clearly that Fátima's house, which used to be Pepe Torres's house, was at once the sanctuary of Diana the Huntress, the convent of martial arts, the yellow dwelling and the hangar of reparations. I can remember it, but I can't see it. I can't see it, and no matter how much time I spend immersing myself in the past, I'm not going to see it.

And so, I've got a new plan, which I hope to initiate soon.

Three weeks ago, they started pruning the trees, and then the truck with the earth arrived. It was driven by a man and a woman; she was driving. I don't know if they're a couple or brother and sister. Their names are Reha and Justin and they don't say much, but they work side by side. So far, they've pruned and tidied the acacias, the palms and the pine tree by the pool. They reminded me that what I thought was a fourth acacia is in fact a false pepper, those ones that drop those little balls that look like pink peppercorns and which you can easily slip on. All those trees were by this point taller than our house. Now that they've been pruned, though, the light comes in directly, at dawn as well as at dusk. It is no longer possible to prolong or extend dusk. I don't know if you remember, but after mid-August, the light changes, and after the sun sets, darkness arrives very quickly. I must be mindful to ensure that the night doesn't catch me out. It's better that way.

The only difficulty they've run into so far has to do with the earth. Reha pointed out that we can't just tip it straight down on to the tiles of the swimming pool, because ultimately the water won't drain and the roots of the fruit trees will rot. I want to plant orange trees. I'm waiting to see if they can get hold of a hydraulic hammer; we might be able to borrow one from a farmer who they work for in the mornings. Last week I pushed the issue, asking when they'd be able to get started, and Justin, without a word, handed me a hammer from his toolbox, as if to say, 'After you.' It's the first time I've seen him smile. The next morning, I climbed down into the swimming pool and knelt on the little hexagonal sky-blue and white tiles, ready to smash them. They are called 'gresite' tiles; that's what they're known as. I remembered Dad once saying, from one year to the next, that a few gresites had come off, and all at once I felt sad and didn't feel able to smash them up with the hammer. *I felt sorry for the gresites.* The previous sentences is, without a doubt, the most ridiculous thing I have ever written. I present to you this image of middle-class neurosis and I'm embarrassed, I'm embarrassed at telling you all these silly things when I know intuitively what you've all been through up there.

The branches have come down and a new horizon has opened up; the terraces have gone back to being spacious balconies looking on to the desert, the mountain and the lights of far-off villages. From the northern terrace you can see the housing development again. The place where the view of the landscape has been cleared the most is the southern terrace, where I have dinner every night, and which looks out on to our street, on to the dark ravine and Gran Vega gleaming beyond. Just behind the ravine and the first few hills I can once again see the train tracks. Every evening I watch the carriages go past that used to take me to Valencia and you to Madrid. I can also make out the fruit groves at the edge of the river, the bridge over the reservoir and its complicated hydraulic geometries; the big motorway to the south is now a vast flowing river fed by various tributaries. I can spend hours watching the little drops of light from the cars and trucks, like satellites on their way to far-off galaxies. Reddish mounds and dun-coloured banks have reappeared to the left of the motorway, and at night they are dotted with isolated lights, which I guess must be little farmsteads or cottages, apart from a cluster of white lights that I have always imagined belong to a little industrial estate, with around six or seven warehouses. When I was about sixteen, I would watch this cluster every night at midnight as minuscule moped headlights criss-crossed it: I would imagine boys and girls with their bikes out there in the small hours, eating sunflower seeds and spraying graffiti slogans amid the silent hangars, beneath the cold lampposts, surrounded by ditches. It's been like a kind of gift; I've been able to see the landscape just as it could be seen in 1997.

Above the railway tracks, the fruit groves, the isolated houses, the industrial estate and the motorway, the horizon line emerges, a hill sharply dotted with five lampposts and which I have always imagined as the last street, with no houses or traffic, on the edge of an unknown residential development that remains hidden behind the mountain. Those five lights recall a constellation in a line, fallen stars, placed there to mark the border between the land and the sky. I could spend many minutes observing them after dinner, trying to make out some silhouette or activity, wondering what is over there. Trying to work out what you can see from there. As you can see, I am devoting myself once again to attaching images of my own invention to this happily recovered landscape. I project myself out in all directions from this renewed vantage point. Looking is a form of travelling. Nevertheless, and here is where I introduce a key plot point, I have decided to travel; I'm going to start a real exploration. I've spent my whole life wanting to know what those lights are, what those houses are like, how midnight feels in that industrial estate. I don't know if it will be feasible, but I would like to get to all the places you can see from our house, from our tower (and I have all the autumn evenings to do it). Now, in the evenings, I sit on the southern terrace (which is actually more south-eastern). With my back to the dusk, I watch how the sky grows dark in oceanic gradations of marine blue. There comes a moment when a mauve colour appears among these ribbons of blue. Every evening the exact same shade. It's not clouds, it's not the air, the sky. It is a colour, a colour that floats on the horizon. As I observe it, I amuse myself by thinking of all the destinations that have opened up, all the places I am going to visit, all the adventures I am going to have.

5th September
Dear, dear brother: happy birthday! Today I'll just write a short message – the people helping me with the earthworks and the vegetable garden are here today and there's still a lot to be done. I'll write more when I have a moment. I have a big update for you . . .

Hugs and kisses to the whole family. And don't forget to send me photos of your celebrations!

12th September

Hey brother, I hope you had a good birthday? Let me know if you guys did anything. I remember you used to hate celebrating it, I don't know if your view on that has changed – do people not celebrate birthdays there, either? Well, I hope you did at least manage to have a bit of a break, I imagine you must have a huge amount on your plate at the moment.

Lots of changes still happening here. We filled in the pool with earth at last and planted the first few saplings. Reha came over with a few friends to give us a hand, and they'd managed to get hold of a hydraulic hammer but – surprise! – there was a power cut and we all ended up down in the pool on our knees, hammering and digging away. It was pretty back-breaking work, not least because I made the most of the extra help by also taking out the dead fruit trees and digging over the plot at the entrance.

Even so, on the Saturday afternoon I managed to slip away and visit the lights, the place that marks the end of the horizon. I drove there. I had to take quite a roundabout route to get to those hills: I went under the motorway via the local road, crossed the river by El Aljarche and drove back along the other side, through pig farms and storehouses, and then took a winding track that went up through big red rocks. Every now and again I would stop the car for a while to observe, from this unknown landscape, our own landscape, our house inserted into these unprecedented perspectives.

I was unbearably happy, like a child who has embarked on a fabulous mission. How can I explain it? I had the sense that I was conquering the summit of a hill that the inhabitants of a village have seen for generations but which no one has ever dared climb. Described like this, it seems tremendously exaggerated, but I'm trying to get across the satisfaction, the subtle euphoria I was feeling as I set foot in a place that was new and that at the same time I had been seeing my whole life, away in the distance.

I had taken a video camera with me and each time I stopped I recorded images of our house embedded there, among the ravine, the hills and the housing development. I had to use the zoom to get our windows and bedrooms clearly in the frame. I was hoping to be able to get to those five lampposts, to the empty highway, to that space I have spent so long imagining, although I was also enjoying how long the journey was taking me; I hoped my arrival there would coincide with the exact light I see from our house, with twilight, with that mauve colour that floats over the horizon, but that would now be floating over me. I drove on up, and just as the first lamppost appeared, I came to a fence cutting off the road and a sentry box. Where was I? I got out of the car and came face to face with two soldiers, who emerged from the cabin to ask what I was doing there. It turns out that what I thought was the edge of another housing development is actually a military camp! It's a site I've not been able to find out anything else about; this is why the road looked so bare along the mountain ridge, this is why there is such an absence of traffic and people. I just managed to glimpse a few barracks behind some pine trees – none of which are visible from our house. I'll ask Néstor if he knows anything.

I nodded goodbye and set off again, but a few metres further down I climbed up to a nearby promontory and was able to get a few shots of our house. As I recorded from the place that I've been observing all these evenings, I imagined my own silhouette, minuscule, seen from home. Through the viewfinder of the camera I could make out, very blurrily and by zooming in as much as possible, the armchair I sit in, and at the same time, I could imagine myself being seen from that armchair, alone and bent over the tripod, a smudge on the hillside. I was only able to get to the first lamppost of the five, but I don't mind; the trip was enlivening. Just reaching the edge of the horizon has turned what before was a flat image into a rugged territory, with new details, nuances and modulations. What I thought was a little road passing through pebbles and shrubs is really a long slope with many curves, which goes past two old quarries, and through high walls of sheer rock, cut to reveal great sections of red and yellow mountain with blue seams. My next goal is to get to the little nocturnal industrial estate – what will I find there? If you like I'll send you screenshots of the recordings I took; I'm going to show them to Mum and Dad next time I go and visit.

But that's not all. Another unexpected thing happened this week. I was in the house making dinner when the doorbell rang. The doorbell! It's the first time there's been an unexpected ring at the door. It was Fátima, come to say goodbye. She and her daughter have decided to leave; they're going to join some other relatives in Copenhagen, just like Mar and Diana did. She will work remotely from there and her daughter has been hired by a Danish firm. She seemed really happy, although she was also trying very hard to seem caring and apologetic; she knows full well that they are leaving for a place I cannot go to. It is by no means far-fetched to feel that they're abandoning those of us who remain. All this I thought later; at the time I congratulated her and wished her the best for the journey. She said she was sorry that we had only spent a short time as neighbours. Since they're going to put the house up for sale, she asked me to let them know if I think of anyone who is interested. I can't think of anyone, of course.

That's all for today, dear brother; this time I'm signing off excited about my future projects and a little distracted by past ones.

With love.

22nd September

That's right, I'm still writing to you, although I don't know if you're the slightest bit interested in what I'm telling you. For a while now I've had the nagging sense that I'm writing these letters to myself...

I went down into the city this week to have dinner with Néstor, who told me he has no idea which battalion the military facility I discovered the other day belongs to; he agrees that it's not part of the parachute brigade, which is quite a bit further down the hillside. He said he would ask his father. I brought him a couple of bottles of wine, and he asked me if everything was OK. I told him I was content and comfortable.

I was on my way back after midnight, and as I joined the main motorway, I realized that I had never covered this stretch of road – the stretch you can see from our house – at that time of day. And then something curious happened to me. I've spent so much time looking out from the southern terrace at the tiny lights of the cars on the motorway, but in that moment I felt like *I* was a light crossing the hill. It was like I was splitting in two: as if my observation point on the terrace was installed in my brain, like an operating system you can't reset, and I were seeing myself from the house, even though I wasn't there. I was driving the car and at the same time I was a headlight, one of the distant headlights I see every night at home. I was a subject and an object at the same time. I was two things. Quite a strange experience, to be at once protagonist and an extra in a scene, an active element in the cosmos I constructed in my daily visions.

When I reached the development, everything was dark; the power cuts are becoming more and more frequent now. I used to love it when the lights went. I would walk through the darkness, and the experience transported me to a remote, medieval time. But the other night, I felt scared and depressed – this, I thought, is how the estate would look if it was permanently empty. Once I was home, sitting on my terrace, the electricity returned: the street lit up with the white, neutral gleam of the LED streetlights, which have always seemed like lights with very little personality to me. I don't know if I'm getting old or if I've always been a bit old, because I miss the old streetlights, the orange mercury vapour lamps. Can you feel nostalgic for a type of light bulb? But I would argue that our street has changed because it's now lit differently. After all, does this not change the character of a place? Around the LED there is no gloom; perhaps this is what offends me – the LED introduces the same high definition, the same clarity without shadow or perspective, without hierarchies or distance, as HD flatscreens. But of course, this isn't the reason for this strength of feeling.

I once wrote that melancholy requires work; perhaps nostalgia is similar. A habit someone instilled in me as a child. I think it's quite likely that nostalgia is learnt, that it's a way of relating to the world, that it's not the case that I miss a specific type of streetlamp. If I had known carbide or oil lamps and seen them replaced by the warm and sleepy mercury vapour lamp, I would have missed what came before too, and that orange light would – perhaps

– have seemed to me a grim, pitiful, miserable light. That's how authoritarian and arbitrary nostalgia is.

I went to the industrial estate, and it was in no way an industrial estate – there were no mopeds, graffiti or silent hangars. It was an old converted windmill whose various outbuildings are being rented out as rural apartments, although there was nobody there when I visited; I didn't see any movement. Once there, I couldn't understand how I had imagined that this cluster of lights was a little compound of industrial warehouses. The reality of this place is so different to what I had imagined that now it is impossible to remember what the space I had invented looked like. When I look now from the terrace in this direction, I can only project the image of those rural apartments with their tiled roofs, surrounded by a sandstone brick wall. Perhaps I should stop doing these excursions, but it's so addictive!

Your mercury vapour brother (who wants to know how you're getting on).

4th November

It's your saint's day! I'm writing to personally wish you a good one, although I'm going to the old people's home later and while I'm there, the three of us will record a video message for you. I'm still doing my usual activities, focusing on the vegetable plot and reading old books and playing video games. The swimming pool's coping is still visible around the edge of where all the saplings are planted, and now I can lie down in my pool of earth, despite the fact that there's still an infestation of mosquitoes and I'm forced to get out, covered from head to toe in bites. I've been invited to dinner a couple of times in the city, but I don't know, I don't feel like going. I still embark on my excursions every evening – by now I've circled the entire southern and south-eastern perimeter, and I've digitized the tapes and taken screenshots of the frames where the house looks most clear; I'm sending you a selection. The western and northern vantages will be harder to do because the horizon is further away, but I have a hankering to do a trip; perhaps when I've gone all the way around the house, I'll discover something, a hatch will open and I'll find some sort of treasure.

Fátima brought me a little gift before she left, a little basket made of wicker or straw, which you can hang on the wall with a little plant pot in it. I've put it in the kitchen with mint in it.

Tomorrow I'm going to try and get an appointment at the doctor's – something strange is happening to me. It doesn't seem serious, or even unpleasant, but I am noticing it more and more each week. I've got something in my eyes.

17th December

I'm done. I'm done with the trips.

I've made a terrible mistake.

18th December

Sorry about the message yesterday, Carlos. I'm writing this first thing, I thought I might have worried you.

Something's happened to me. Or perhaps it's more precise to say that I have done something – something that's quite hard to explain. I should have pressed pause on the trips, but I didn't. I carried on exploring, despite sensing that something wasn't right. Perhaps you can tell me why I insisted on not leaving a single spot on the horizon unvisited, why I insisted on recording it all. It doesn't even seem like something I would do – wasn't it you, out of the two of us, who was the more dogged, the one who never gave up? I was the one who grew tired of things and left them half finished. Maybe I was trying to be like you?

I haven't been to the doctor's either; I'm not going to go – the thing I've got in my eyes or my brain doesn't seem to be clinically recognizable at all, it can't even be considered a disorder or an ailment. To me, it feels like a curse, a condemnation. Yes, that's it – I have condemned myself. I have condemned myself and I have condemned this place in its entirety. Over these months I have visited each and every one of the places you can see from our house and, once there, I looked in the direction of our house. I could have focused on looking further, off in other directions, at new horizons, and seeing what new territories opened up around me. What can you see from the place that is seen? But the fact is that I focused on our house.

I have a hundred shots of our house taken from a hundred distinct spots: I traversed the entire panorama, the circumference, covering all four points of the compass. And in this process, everything from before has disappeared. By visiting in person, by *peering at,* then *appearing in,* each visual landmark, I have banished the previous illusions, the landscapes I had invented for this space. Landscapes that I had been inventing since the age of ten, when I spent my first summer at this house. Now, when I look out and survey the landscape from the terrace, I know firsthand what there is in each point of the landscape because I have been out and *surveyed* the terrain (forgive me this play on words). Everything from before, my imagined visual memory, has dissolved without a trace and I feel I have lost something very valuable, something that I ought to have protected but that I have voluntarily and systematically destroyed.

I have annihilated this territory; that is, I have annihilated its memory, and what's more, I didn't rest until I had destroyed it all. I exhausted this landscape; I have erased it. With the naïve excuse of exploring that which had always been an unknown promise, I have ended up erasing the memory of that promise. Or, rather, reality has erased my imagination – has erased me. The world reserves a special severity for punishing the naïve.

Perhaps I'm being a little dramatic. I imagine these woes won't seem like such a big deal to you, and you're probably right. I just have to adapt to this new reality, an unambiguous reality, and construct something new on top of it.

But there is a second factor that is, this time inarguably, unbearably unpleasant. Because I have observed, so painstakingly, the house from all these places, because I have focused on it and, as if that weren't enough, have recorded and photographed it, I now have an incredibly clear memory of how the house looks from all the places that surround me. I don't know why, I really don't know why, I don't know if it has awoken something in my brain, but now, whenever I look outside, the house appears to me just as it looks from the place I am looking at. When I write that it appears to me, I mean that I *see it.* I see it. If I look in the other direction – that is, if, instead of my gaze landing on the streetlights on the hill, it lands on the train tracks – I see the house just as it can be seen from that point on the train tracks. I can no longer get these images out of my mind. And it's not that the house is substituted by the image from that place, but rather that I see the two images at the same time: I see the tracks and I see the house at the same time. It's not that I see the images superimposed on each other or flickering in and out; no – *I see them at the same time.* No matter where I look, I see the house, and I have the sensation that the house is pursuing me. Wherever I look, I see what can be seen from the place I am looking at. And it is unpleasant, it is unbearable, it is a kind of exhausting, dizzying visual dance, like a strobe light bombarding my retina. It gives me migraines and vertigo, real vertigo, like when you have to lie down in bed because the floor is constantly moving all around you.

I don't know if I'm making any sense, but I need to put it down in writing, and if I don't tell *you*, who else am I going to tell? Now I go out on to the balcony with my head bowed, looking at the floor, to avoid this reflective projection, this double landscape.

All the things I could have done, all the projects I could have started, and instead I've spent my time erasing the reasons I wanted to live here. Never have I felt more hopelessly trapped inside this house. My head's been all over the place for days now. I sleep deeply, without dreams, but I don't rest. I try to focus on the vegetable plot and the watering, but I get distracted, the minutes go by and I don't know what I've done, I just stand and stare into space. Whenever I go outside I remember that I'm surrounded by all these duplicated landscapes and I feel constantly called by them, tempted to go back and take another look, in case this thing I have, this anomaly, might have abated. And so I look, and it is always there, awaiting me, the double projection. I wonder if I ought to force myself not to look at the landscape for at least a few weeks so as to cleanse myself, but what do I mean, cleanse – cleanse what? My vision? My neural networks?

In the end, I am almost always overcome by curiosity and anxiety, and so I look again, again and again. I've taken to keeping the blinds drawn, so that this horizon I insisted so obstinately on extending by pruning the trees does not enter the house. But it is oppressive being shut up in a dark house, and so after a few hours I open the blinds and there it is. It is impossible to escape from the landscape. Now I pray that the trees will grow back and conceal the house once more.

I can no longer read, or get through a film or a series, without getting distracted and looking around me; it doesn't matter if it's a full-length film or episodes I've never seen before: it's the same, I get sidetracked and start thinking about everything that's happened to get to this point, I go over and over the events of my life, the decisions I took, the opportunities I failed to take advantage of. I don't reach any kind of conclusion, either, and so eventually I end up staring at the sky or the birds flying overhead or anything, trying not to think about anything, but plagued by a constant swarm of images, landscapes, people from the past. I can no longer be in one place.

The only thing that holds my focus is video games. They demand all of your attention; the virtual space holds sway over your gaze. I don't even need new ones, or particularly sophisticated storylines; I can happily play games I've already completed, that I've already moved about in thousands of times, I don't care. Even though I know what is waiting for me in each session, I have to be attentive, alert. In these games, the world is an understandable object. They offer a realm of certainty, where everything is coordinated and repeated in the same fashion, and the rules neatly organize and allocate everything in the game, in the world. The only thing that messes it up for me are the power cuts, of course, which are more and more frequent. When this happens, I go to the pool, lie down on the ground and look up at the sky. The cuts are affecting an ever-greater spread of towns and districts, and so the light pollution disappears, the glow disappears and the star-studded darkness of the sky reappears. Sometimes it seems as if I might succeed in actually seeing you, or that you might succeed in seeing me.

Goodbye from your starry-eyed brother.

24th December

Hello, dear family, I'm sending you greetings on behalf of our parents. They're asking you to send us lots of photos of the past few days. We're wondering what you think of these snap elections. How do our public affairs look from up there?

Tomorrow I'm going to Valencia for a week to see some old friends. My problem hasn't let up, but I hope that going away for a few days will help quieten it down a little.

Happy Christmas, Carlos.

14th March

Dear Carlos, thank you for your last email. I've been wanting to write to you for a few weeks now, but the fact is that, without realizing it, I've been busier than I thought I'd be. The back-to-back power cuts have forced me to go into town more. We're organizing ourselves into little collectives to buy generators. I cycle everywhere now – petrol is scarce, and we need it to produce electricity. Thanks to Reha and her brother I've been able to get in touch with the family who moved into Fátima's house; they've got three children, and there are two teenagers, a nephew and a niece, called Carlos and Selena, who also live with them. If we manage to get a third family to come and live in the house by the tennis courts, we'll be able to live reasonably well, sharing the generator between the three houses. They've organized demonstrations in the city; I can't go because of my record, but I try and lend a hand with the logistics, getting food supplies together, that sort of thing. In the end, what with sorting things out with the neighbours and my weekly trips to the village, I've ended up helping out with some extra tuition a few afternoons here and there, for my younger neighbours as well as Reha and Justin's little sisters. It's not bad, actually. I needed to feel useful. The fruit trees and vegetables aren't doing so well, due to the water restrictions, but I'm not complaining – I produce enough to give things away to my new friends in town. I can't see myself setting up a stall in the market, but in exchange for my oranges, lemons, figs and apricots, I receive other foodstuffs such as eggs and vegetables, or help when something breaks. I've also sold some furniture and appliances, like the fridge-freezer, which was enormous and used too much electricity. I'm not ruling out renting out rooms in the future, but I don't want to make too many plans, either. No more plans.

My visual duplication or 'walling in', as I sometimes call it, hasn't eased, but I have slowly got used to it. When I got back from Valencia everything was exactly as I had left it. There were a few heavy weeks when I thought about leaving, until I realized I had nowhere else to go. So, I shut myself up with the video games, until one night, one of the power cuts lasted longer than usual. Tired and anxious, I went out on to the balcony and there you all were. There was no question it was you I was seeing, it had to be you. You have dozens of power plants, we hear; I guess that in the last few months of so much activity you've grown.

I also realized that I've been going about it all wrong this whole time. I feel a bit daft, but I always used to look for you when there was a full moon, when, obviously, it's in your night, when it's a new moon, that I can best see your cities. Such an elemental detail, and it hadn't occurred to me. I felt like buying a telescope, but then I realized we have one, small but functional, from when we were children and were given the AstroNova. What with the constant light restrictions I don't even have to rely on the power cuts any more to see the night sky reappear. There are also rumours that people are leaving and heading wherever they can. Whatever the reason, the nearby cities don't shine as brightly any more. Before it was the earth that illuminated the sky, and now, little by little, we're being illuminated from our sky – or your sky – once again. I thank you all, I am thankful that you are there every night. Because it is a relief, for lots of reasons. I have a new vanishing point.

I place the telescope on the upstairs terrace and I can cross all that space and scour the different sectors of the lunar colony; sometimes I think that I can make out the hives, the power plants, the labs and the aerodromes, but for that I'd need a new, bigger telescope. I suppose there are military bases, too, but these, as we have learnt, do not show up on maps.

If I'm feeling especially dreamy or fanciful I allow myself to be carried away by the emotion, and I imagine that one of those tiny lights is your house, shining away up there. As I observe you all, I realize that this landscape that surrounds me is also evolving and changing; before long the five streetlights on the horizon will no longer come on at night, some of the houses will disappear and others will come in their place, and the land that surrounds me will once more conceal hidden meanings. On other nights I lie down in the swimming pool of earth and wonder what it would be like to live inside a crater, a sea of earth framed by slopes and gorges, and I wonder if this earthen pond, still encircled by what was the white cement edge of the swimming pool, is not also a crater.

Yours, your most nocturnal, terrestrial brother.

7th May

Yesterday I went for a walk, and I remembered something. Do you remember the evening we were with Dad and we were walking really fast up a hill, trying to catch the sunset? I think it was at the beach, by Grandma's house. I don't remember where Mum was that evening, but Dad wanted to record the sunset with his video camera and we were late. I want to say that he was carrying you on his shoulders. I don't know if we got there in time or not, but I do remember that I was really sad at the idea of not seeing the sunset, I was sad at the simple possibility of missing out on this promise. Do you remember? I thought of it because even today I get a kind of anxious jumpiness when it starts to grow dark and I'm not in the right place to see it. I've always had this, as if I were losing out on something incredibly precious that I've been waiting the whole day for. It's not serious, it's fine if I'm working, teaching, or just tied up at that time of day, but a slight unease comes over me if I am at home and it starts to grow dark and I don't see the sun as it sets. It seems as if over the years, sadness turns into anxiety, don't you think?

That was the last email. I stood up with a heavy, sad feeling and went over to the window. Tomorrow I will sit down and calmly write to him. If only I could see him again; if only I could embrace him, but all I can do is turn off the light and look at the sky and imagine that he's watching me from up there, from Earth. Here we never look at the sky, because the sky is somehow the past. I listen to the ticking of the clock and my sleeping family breathing, but I'm not tired, and I can't go to bed now. So, I stay by the window, looking up at the sky, on my Moon of earth, down below him, and yet forever suspended before his eyes. And so we both remain, looking upwards, each one of us the other's sky.

Mare Imbrium, sector 2, July 2035

Acknowledgements

This book is dedicated to my parents, Esther and Luis, who throughout their lives made possible a home that included a great number of different kinds of people.

When I finished the first chapter, in April 2020, I was surprised to realize that nine years had passed since finishing my previous project at the end of 2011. I suppose this book is a record of, and a homage to, all the people who left us from this year on, and whose presence, at times sporadic, at times far too distant, has accompanied me throughout this period.

I am grateful to many people for their care, advice and kindness. First, I would like to offer my thanks to the people I lived with and who supported me as I was writing throughout 2020 and 2021, in flats and houses in Madrid, Las Torres de Cotillas and Águilas: Rebeca Amieva, my parents, my aunt Encarni López and my cousin Ana Huertas. The latter I also have to thank for being my consultant on matters of diagnostic techniques in small cats.

The careful, close reading that my brother Carlos and my other brother, Javier Fernández, gave the work helped to define and improve the original manuscript (they also assuaged many of the worries I'd had about the book until that point). Another old friend, Andrea Toribio, also read the book rigorously, and her comments and corrections were essential to finding its tone. This novel belongs to all of you, too.

I have been lucky enough in my life to know two people whose work I admire and who over time I have come to admire and love for their friendship. The first is Luis Magrinyà, whose chapter 'Luxor' inspired in large part the tone, perspective and sense of distance in 'Ocean of Light'. Whenever I felt I was losing my footing during the writing process, Luis advised and reassured me. The novel found its title thanks to him.

The second is Gonzalo Torné, whose encouragement, dedication and invaluable generosity made it possible for the book to come this far. He has always been there when I needed him.

While I was writing this novel, a pandemic was happening; we were experiencing difficult times, and my life underwent profound changes. I am convinced that friendship is what kept us alive, or, at the very least, far from harm. Finally, then, my deep gratitude to Lorena Iglesias, Julián Génisson, Ion de Sosa, Miquel Insua and Sergio Jiménez for their warmth, their care and their friendship.

And above all, and in particular, I would like to thank and to celebrate Natalia Marín – her loyalty, joy and love.

Madrid, September 2023